# The Beauty Queen

The Adventures of Silver Dove, Book Five

## Eliza Scalia

Cover Illustration by:
Wayne F. Shurtz and Cheyanne and Jean Buffkin
Based upon the characters originally designed by Suji Gallianetti

Dedicated to BJ Storey, a songwriter from my class on Evaluation and Assessment of the Individual in 2019. He was kind enough to write Luis' song within this story. He wrote it in less than ten minutes, a very impressive writer. This is also dedicated to Syndi Hernandez- Sluka, who gave me inspiration for this story by telling me her daughter's story, a story very similar to the Beauty Queen.

# <u>Chapter One</u>
## Colomba- Preparing for the Fair

My hands busily mix together some ingredients in a bowl to make a pie while my grandmother is clearing some room in the fridge to place the uncooked pie in. We will be baking tomorrow while doing all the prep work today. A smile of excitement is on my flour covered face as I start adding more ingredients into my mixture. Right now, my grandmother and I are preparing some cookies and pies that we will be entering in the county fair contests. Every year at the end of summer vacation the town has a county fair where there are rides, games, and a bunch of contests. The contests usually involve contests for baking, handmade items, and farming. My grandmother and I always enter some of our baked goods as well as some things we have knitted or sewn and we always end up winning at least a few ribbons.

As my grandmother finishes arranging a pie crust in the pie plate, she turns her attention to me.

"Did you hear about the new contest they plan on having this year?"

"No Nonna, what is it?"

"It's a beauty contest. You should enter, you could easily win." I smile at my grandmother's compliment, but there still lies a feeling of discomfort in me.

"No thank you. I have never liked contests like that. I don't think girls should be put on display to look pretty. It just doesn't feel right." My grandmother nods her head, understanding what I mean.

"Yes, I can see why you would say that. I just thought that you might have some fun with it. Apparently, they are also going to have a large cash prize for the winner. I'm going to bet that a lot of girls in the town are going to try and enter." I lower my gaze, suddenly feeling a bit sick.

"Yeah, I bet a lot of them will." At school, I constantly hear girls talking about their appearance. They are always complaining about how their hair looks, how they are too fat, how they wish their nose was a different size, and countless other complaints. They are always trying to make themselves look beautiful while constantly pointing out their own flaws. A lot of girls enter contests like this to make themselves feel better about themselves. They want to win so that they can feel beautiful. When they lose they believe they are ugly.

I have never really understood why other girls are so obsessed with how they look. Whenever

I get myself ready for the day, I just make myself look and dress the way I want to, not what everyone else thinks is fashionable. Most people think that I dress a bit old fashioned, but it's what I like and that's what matters. I know that in many ways I could be considered unusual, but when it comes to stuff like this, I'm glad that I am.

Bringing my mixing bowl over to the pie crust my grandmother just prepared, I scoop my mixture into the pie crust. It is kind of a creepy looking mixture that looks like some kind of blob that would eat people in those old scary movies. When it is baked through it will taste wonderful as a mixed berry pie. My grandmother and I always win first prize when it comes to our baking. We kick major butt at baking.

Glancing outside the kitchen window, I look out at the garden enjoying the beauty of late summer. I know that a lot of the people my age hate this time of year since that means that their summer vacation is about to end. I'm not one of these people though. I am super excited to start school again in about two weeks. I will be starting my sophomore year of high school and I can't wait to get back. I miss seeing my friends every day and having some excitement. Summer is great at first, but after a while you start running out of things to do.

I smile when I think about something else related to school. I haven't seen the Crow in months. The last time I saw him was when he gave powers to a girl named Rosie and transformed her into the Black Iris. After that he just sort of disappeared for the rest of the school year. Nobody really knows where he's gone, but I don't really care just as long as I don't have to deal with him anymore. His fan club seemed extremely upset that he is no longer here, but everybody else has been so happy to not see him.

Since I haven't had to deal with him for a while, I've been able to spend my time as Silver Dove doing some stuff superheroes should be doing. I have been stopping bad guys in my town, and the other towns around mine, and trying to make this world a better place. That's what every person should try to do, to make the world a better place, but having superpowers just makes that goal a bit easier.

Sometimes I stop to wonder where the Crow has gone, but then I push that thought out of my mind. I shouldn't care about the Crow at all. Yes, we are supposed to be allies since we both wear the pins that give us our powers, but he was the one who decided to go against me and create chaos in our school. I'm glad he's gone. I hope he never comes back. I hope that he will give his pin to someone who deserves it. Someone who will use it like I have. Someone who will try and make the world a better place. I can only hope that he has done that, but he probably hasn't. A power-hungry looney like him will probably hang on to it until he is dead and then somebody will have to pry the pin from his cold dead hands. Eww, I just grossed myself out with that thought.

As I finish up placing the top crust on the pie and pressing down around the edges, I place the pie in the fridge so that it will be ready to bake tomorrow. My grandma and I start cleaning up while I anxiously look at the clock. In about an hour I'm going to be meeting up with some friends of mine, Nat and Luis, to hang out at a local diner where all the people our age go to hang out and eat some greasy food. It's an awesome place.

I scrub down the counter impatiently with a soapy sponge as I try to make time move faster with my mind. Out of all the cool superpowers I got out of the pin, why couldn't I get control over time too? That would really come in handy. Oh well, I guess we all have to go through the boring moments of the day, even those of us with superpowers.

# Chapter Two
## Luis-
## A Brand New
## Start

I'm sitting across from Colomba in a booth table in the crowded diner called The Captain's Ship. Apparently, the guy who runs the place used to be a Captain in the Navy or something, I'm not sure but that's what I heard.

Nat is eating a hamburger beside Colomba, while Colomba nibbles on some french fries as she tells us about how she and her grandmother are entering some stuff that they have made in the county fair. She and her grandmother have won many ribbons at the fair before and she is anxious to win a few more this year.

As she talks, I am struck speechless. In her excitement, her smile is huge and her eyes are lit up, making her even prettier than usual. Her bright aquamarine eyes seem to shine like jewels even in the dim light of this diner. It feels strange that only a few months ago she and I didn't even speak. I had been avoiding her because of something that happened with Alex, and when I did start talking to her she started avoiding me because Alex told her that I am the Crow. We got everything worked out though and we are just as good of friends as ever. I felt pretty bad having to lie to her about being the Crow. I do want to tell her one day, but for right now I can't. She absolutely hates the Crow right now. I just need to make her realize that the Crow is the good guy here and then I can tell her.

I decided something a few months ago though because of everything that had happened. I decided that the Crow was going to take a little break. I was going to give everyone a chance to miss me before I come back. And miss me they have. The bullying in the school seems to have gotten worse than ever and all of the bullied kids are practically begging for me to come back. Begging me to transform them into my next soldier so that they can get their revenge. Once the new school year starts, I may just do that. I don't want to disappoint all of the other bullied kids who look up to me. I know that I need to come back. I just need to find the right moment to show my face again. The only problem is that I have no idea when that perfect moment will come. For now though, I will just enjoy the moment. I look at Colomba as Nat tells her about some of the rides at the fair that she wants to go on.

Man, I wish I could tell Colomba how I really feel about her. I have had the biggest crush on her ever since I first met her the first day of freshman year. It's hard to believe that was almost a year ago. It all feels like it has flown by. Nat already knows how I feel, she said it straight to my face once. Every now and again she tells me that I should tell Colomba, but I can't do that now. Right now, I am still seen as the loser of the school. I can't bring myself to ask her out now or else she would say no. I mean who would agree to go out with the biggest loser in school? I need to wait until I have finally won as the Crow. Then I won't have to worry about being seen as a loser because then people will be too scared to make fun of me. They will be so afraid of the Crow transforming another bullied kid that they won't bully anyone ever again. If Silver Dove had just stayed out of my way I might have already succeeded by now.

I had been so busy getting wrapped up in my own thoughts that I didn't notice that Colomba asked me something. She and Nat are now staring at me expectantly.

"I'm sorry Colomba, what did you say?" She chuckles before she repeats her question.

"I asked if you were going to enter some of your artwork in the county fair. They have competitions for drawings, paintings, and other artistic stuff. I know that you can win something there. You are such an amazing artist." I can feel my face growing warm and I know that I'm blushing like an idiot from her compliment.

"Well I don't know about that…" I have been drawing ever since I can remember, but I have only ever shown my drawings to my art teacher, Mr. Sizemore, Uncle Diego, Nat, and Colomba. I have never shown them to anybody else, and the thought of putting them in a contest almost makes me want to puke in fear.

"Oh come on Luis. You could beat anybody there with your hands tied behind your back. You've got nothing to be nervous about." Nat says this with complete confidence. She is usually very shy around most people, but whenever she is around her friends she says whatever she pleases without any fear. It's almost funny to see her suddenly change from super shy to extremely confident.

"I've just never… never really shown my stuff to many people before, let alone put it in a contest." Colomba seems to notice something behind me since her eyes quickly focus on something and a smile lights up her face.

"Hold on a second." She gets out of the booth and goes over to the diner counter to pick up a piece of paper from a pile next to the register. Colomba comes back over and hands me the paper before she sits back down, but not next to Nat like she was before, she sits right next to me. She is so close to me right now that our arms are just touching each other's. Even though we are already close, I want to move closer. "I saw that when we were coming in, thought it might help you make your decision." I glance down at the paper to see that it is a list of all the competitions at the county fair. My eyes are immediately drawn to the section of the list that talks about the art competitions. Colomba points at one entry on the list.

"Look, right here there is a contest for drawings of animals. You could enter that drawing of that crow you did near the beginning of last year that you did for art class. And here's another contest for drawing a landscape. You could use that picture of a field with the tree in it that you showed me. You could definitely win a ribbon or two from what I've seen you do." I smile at her words as my eyes scan through the list. My eyes stop when I look at what's at the top of the list. In bold print is the contest for a portrait. I point at it.

"What's up with this one? Why is it in bold print like that? Is that one important or something?" Colomba looks at where I am pointing and nods her head.

"Oh yeah. The portrait competition is always the biggest one in the art category. All of the competitions have a small prize, just a few bucks, but since the portrait competition is so popular they have a much bigger cash prize for that. I think you get around a hundred dollars if you win. I think you could do really well at that one too. I've never seen you draw a person before, but I know you'll do great." My eyes grow wide at being able to win that much. If I win, I could buy that set of paint brushes and paints I was looking at the other day. I have been thinking about getting into painting for a while, but it is a bit more expensive than just drawing like I usually do. My heart sinks in my chest when I see something else listed on the paper.

"It says here though that I would have to turn everything in by the day after tomorrow. It would be hard to get everything organized and draw something new too. I'm not sure if I can do a portrait in one day." Colomba looks sad for a moment before she looks up at me questioningly.

"What would make it difficult? I'll help if I can." I smile at her willingness to help me.

"Well, I already have some colored pencils as well as regular pencils and a large sketch pad, so I have what I need to draw the portrait. The problem would be to find someone willing to spend practically all day, holding still, so that I can draw them as well as find a place to do it so that the background of the portrait looks nice." Colomba's sad expression immediately fades into a warm smile.

"That's not a problem at all. I'd be happy to do that for you." I look at her with shock.

"Really?" She chuckles at my disbelief.

"Of course, we can do it in my backyard if you want. There's a lot of beautiful scenery there so I think it would turn out great." The biggest smile spreads across my face. She is willing to spend all day with me tomorrow just to help me out? She really does care about me.

"Are you sure? You said that you would be finishing up baking all that stuff tomorrow for the contests."

"Oh, don't worry about that. We have all that stuff prepared, we just need to put it in the oven and I'm sure my grandmother can do it while we work outside." My smile is so big right now that it is actually making my face ache, but I don't care.

"Okay then, we should probably start early so we can get it done, Can I come over at around eight?" She nods her head and writes her address down on a napkin, which I quickly put in my pocket since I see someone I recognize come through the front door. Someone I was hoping I wouldn't see until the school year started, Alex.

Alex smiles when he sees Colomba sitting at the table. His smile falters for a moment though when he sees that she is sitting very close to me. He quickly returns his smile to his face and walks over to our table.

"Hey there guys. Mind if I join you?" I want to tell him that yes I do mind, but I don't want to look like a jerk in front of Colomba and Nat.

"Sure. Sit down Alex." Colomba states with a smile on her face, but I feel better when I don't hear any enthusiasm in her voice. Instead of sitting in the empty spot next to Nat, he surprises all of us by scooching in beside Colomba. To make him fit, she and I have to both move over and I am almost pressed against the wall. A silent moment of tension seems to pass between Alex and I with Colomba in between us. Nat looks at Alex and I curiously, but she doesn't say anything. I know that she knows that I like Colomba, but I think she has just noticed how much Alex likes her too, she can see the competition between the two of us.

"So what are you guys looking so excited about?" Alex says this to everyone, but his eyes are only on Colomba.

"We just finished convincing Luis to enter a few of the contests at the county fair." Colomba states with an innocent smile. For a moment, it looks like Alex will say something mean to me about that, but then he remembers who else is with him so he holds his tongue.

"That sounds pretty exciting. What

contests are you thinking about doing?" Even though he says it sounds exciting, it sounds like he doesn't care at all.

"I'm going to be trying to do a few of the art competitions." I don't say very much but that doesn't matter to Alex. It seems to be all he needs. I know him all too well, so I recognize the happiness in his eyes that tells him that I have given him more ammo to tease me with. Just to make things worse, Colomba leaves me alone with Alex using one simple statement.

"Yeah, he's even going to be drawing my portrait tomorrow for one of the competitions." The happy glow in Alex's eyes just seems to grow brighter at that comment, leaving a cold feeling in the pit of my stomach. "If you guys will excuse me a moment, I'm going to go to the ladies' room." Nat seems to perk up at these words.

"I'll go with you." Alex steps out of the booth so that Colomba can get out and she and Nat head to the bathroom, leaving me alone with Alex. Why do girls always go to the bathroom in groups? It's weird, but I guess I'll never understand women so I'm okay with that. What I'm not okay with though is that they left me here alone with Alex. Alex sees this and a cruel smile plays across his lips. I can feel my hand automatically going toward my Crow Medal that I have pinned on the shirt underneath my hoodie. Even though I haven't shown myself as the Crow for a while now, I still keep the medal on me all the time. I guess I wear it so much even though I know I'm not going to use it because it makes me feel safer when I do have it. I can't use it right now, but it makes me feel better knowing that if I needed to I could take Alex down. Alex lets the silence hang between us for a moment, letting me start to get worried, wondering what he's planning on doing.

"So, you're going to be drawing her?" My eyes narrow as I glare at him.

"Yeah, I am." Alex chuckles at me as he takes a few french fries off my plate and eats them.

"I bet you had to beg her for that. Imagine, having a no talent loser like you sketching her all day. Sounds like torture to me." Now it is my turn to chuckle at him.

"Actually, she offered to model for me and even invited me to her house to do it. She says that she would be happy to do it since she thinks that I am such a good artist." Alex's smile falters for a moment before it returns.

"Yeah right. Why would she want to hang out with you all day?" I chuckle again.

"Well I'm hanging out with her now, aren't I? She was the one who invited me to come, but she didn't invite you." Alex's smile disappears completely, and he slowly turns to glare at me. I had only said that out loud because I had felt so confident since Colomba had agreed to help me and I had my hand close to my medal, which always makes me feel better. I should have kept a grip on myself though since I know now that I'm totally dead.

"Even if you have a hot girl like her to model for you, your drawing still won't win. Who would pick the drawing of a no talent loser like you as the winner? I mean, you're not even that good at drawing." My hands ball into fists on top of the table. Really? I'm not the good artist? He thinks that I won't win? I have seen his drawings in the art class we were in together. He is terrible while the teacher always praised my work. I could see the looks of jealousy on Alex's face whenever the teacher would compliment me. He knows how good I am. He is lying to me now.

I want to say something cruel back to him, but I am saved from making that dumb mistake since Colomba and Nat return to the table. Nat lowers her gaze when she sees Alex. She has known Alex for a while since he is always trying to be around Colomba, but apparently she still doesn't feel very comfortable around him. I think she can sense what he is truly like. Something that he hides very well while he's around Colomba.

"Hello boys. Did we miss anything interesting? A fight to the death, a nuclear holocaust, perhaps dolphins taking over the world?" I can't help but smile at Colomba's remark while Alex gets up from the table.

"Not much, but I'm afraid that I have to go. I need to do a few things before the day is over. See you guys later." I hold back a sigh of relief as he leaves the restaurant and Colomba sits down beside me again. The three of us talk and laugh before we all have to head home about an hour later.

Now that I am sitting at home at my desk in my room, I take another look at the paper in my hand that lists all the contests. I almost can't believe that I'm doing this. I can't believe that I'm actually going to be entering my art in the county fair. I already have several of my pieces laying out in front of me on top of my desk that I will be entering in the contests. I have two drawings here, plus I will have the portrait I'm doing tomorrow.

My eyes scan further down the list of contests, but my eyes stop when I see something that I'm kind of interested in. One of the contests listed is a song writing competition. I have always been interested in music and I always thought that it would be cool to be able to write a song. Maybe I should try to enter that contest too. It might be fun.

When I look at the clock, I see that it is getting pretty late and Colomba and I agreed to meet early in the morning so I need to get my sleep. I turn off my light and bury myself underneath my covers, eagerly waiting for the sun to rise so that I can draw Colomba's portrait.

# Chapter Three
## Colomba-
## Dark Thoughts
## On A Happy Day

Nat and I leave Luis and Alex at the table behind us as we head into the girl's bathroom in The Captain's Ship. My gosh that was so uncomfortable. As soon as Alex had stepped into the restaurant it felt as if all the air in the room had been sucked out. Nat and Luis had looked a bit uncomfortable when he sat down too, especially Luis though. When he saw Alex, his eyes looked like the eyes of a rabbit being cornered by a wolf. I let Alex sit with us only out of politeness, expecting him to sit in the vacant seat beside Nat, but he instead sat next to me and Luis, leaving me to be smooshed in between the two of them.

When I was in between the two of them, it almost felt like the two of them wanted to beat each other up and the only thing stopping them from doing that was me sitting in between them. I actually told them that I was going to the girl's bathroom because I wanted to get away. I don't even have to go. As soon as Nat and I are alone in the bathroom, I lean against the sink counter and let out a sigh of relief.

"Man, that felt really uncomfortable. It felt as if I was the middle of the sandwich between those two." Nat nods at me as she leans against the counter beside me.

"I know. It looked as if they were trying to crush you or something."

"Why do you think Alex did that, sit beside me like that even though there was no room?" Nat chuckles.

"Birdy, you are sometimes so blind to the obvious that it's pretty hilarious." She laughs a bit more while I feel my face growing warm in embarrassment.

"Well thanks, that really makes me feel a lot better." She has to force herself to stop laughing before she speaks again.

"I'm sorry Birdy, but it's true. It's obvious to everyone, but you, that the two of them like you." It takes all of my self-control to not roll my eyes. I already know that Alex likes me, he compliments me all the time and is always trying to get close to me, but Luis is just a friend. Nat has told me multiple times that she thinks that Luis likes me, but I'm sure it's not true. He is one of my best friends and I don't think he will ever have feelings like that for me.

My heart sinks in my chest when I think about something that Luis had told me a few months ago. He said that Alex only likes me because he thinks I'm pretty. He said that Alex doesn't really care about me as a person at all. I have to hide the pain I am feeling from Nat so that she doesn't get worried. Alex is my friend. He has been so kind to me ever since we met. I'm sure that he would still care about me even if I wasn't pretty. I'm sure of it.

"Thanks for that bit of news Nat, but you've already told me that a million times." She chuckles at me before she suddenly becomes very serious.

"Birdy I feel like I need to tell you this, but I don't think you'll like it." I look at her, suddenly feeling very confused.

"Nat you know you can tell me anything. What's on your mind?" She stares down at the tile floor and twirls her braids around her finger. This is what she always does whenever she feels nervous about something.

"I think you should avoid Alex." My heart that had felt like it was sinking in my chest a moment ago is now beating rapidly in my chest as the shock courses through me.

"What are you talking about?" She avoids my gaze as she continues talking.

"I've been hearing a lot of stuff about Alex ever since we started going to school with him almost a year ago and I think he's just bad news. I've heard a lot of people talk about terrible stuff he's done to other people. Sometimes he doesn't even have a reason for doing mean things to others. He just does it for fun. He may be nice to you now, but if you get any closer to him he might change. I think we should just avoid him until he gets the hint. I mean, we both can clearly see that he wants to date you. If we avoid him he'll get the hint that you don't want to date him. You don't want to, right?" Nat looks at me with a worried expression. From the face she's making, I know that she's worried that I will say that I am interested. I do not disappoint her.

"No. I am definitely not interested in that. I told you that I don't want to date while we're in high school. I want to focus on school so that I can get good grades and go to college." Nat's serious expression disappears immediately as she smiles warmly at me.

"You know, you can have a little fun while still get good grades. It's not impossible to do both." I smile back at her.

"Good to know. We can talk more about that later though. Let's go back to the table before the boys start missing us too much." We both walk out of the bathroom and even though I am smiling, my mind is racing with dark thoughts.

So, Nat doesn't think I should trust Alex too? Not too long ago, Luis tried to warn me about Alex as well. I didn't listen to him then since Alex had told me that Luis was the Crow and I thought he was just trying to make excuses for why I shouldn't believe what Alex said. Maybe Alex did see the Crow transform and it was just somebody that looks like Luis, or he was lying, I don't know. Now though, I think that Luis may have a point. Alex always seems to have power over everybody. Most people try to avoid him in the hallway and they always look uncomfortable whenever I say that I am friends with him. My own grandmother says that I should avoid him. She hasn't even met him before, but from what I have said about him, she doesn't trust him. Maybe I should just believe what they have told me and avoid him.

The only problem though is that Alex is kind to me. I don't want to be unkind to someone if they are being kind to me. That's just a horrible thing to do to someone. My father and grandmother always taught me to be kind to others. I have always tried to follow that advice in life and I don't want to give up on it now. Why have values in life if you're not going to follow them? I am starting to understand what everyone has been trying to tell me, but I don't know what I can do about it.

When we make it back to the table, Alex surprisingly saves all of us from feeling uncomfortable by saying that he has to head home. As he leaves though, I detect a bit more tension between him and Luis than what had been there since I left the table. Did something happen with those two while Nat and I were in the bathroom? When the remaining three of us start a conversation, Luis doesn't explain, and I don't ask. If he doesn't want to talk about what happened then I will not push it.

We talk for a little while longer before we all have to head home. As soon as I make it to my house I rush to my room and start looking for something to wear tomorrow. If Luis is going to put in all that effort and time to do my portrait, I want to look my best. After what feels like ages of searching, I settle on a simple white dress that I usually only wear to church. I finish a few of my chores before heading to bed with a smile on my face, knowing that I will be doing something good for Luis.

# Chapter Four
## Luis-
## The Portrait

Okay, just breathe. Breathe and everything will be okay. I keep repeating that in my head as I get ready to go over to Colomba's house. My uncle will be driving me there in just a couple minutes. I am spending that time looking at myself in the mirror while Shadow watches me with an amused glance. My hands quiver a little in my nervousness as I fiddle with the sleeves of my shirt.

"You need to calm yourself down Master or else you will never be able to hold your pencil with that shaking hand." Shadow says with a chuckle in her voice. I can't help but smile at her words.

"Thanks, that's a real help." I pick off a few pieces of lint on my shirt before I turn around to face her. "How do I look?" I am wearing a solid black T-shirt and dark jeans. I thought it would make me look cool. I mean black is a cool color, right? Shadow chuckles again.

"You look fine."

"Are you sure?" I look down at myself

again, trying to find anything wrong.

"Trust me Master you look good. I should know. Underneath all these feathers I am still a girl you know." I lower my head, suddenly realizing something. I don't really know anything about Shadow at all. All we ever really talk about is me; my mission as the Crow, my problems, and things that have happened in my life. I don't even know the basic stuff about her. I don't know how old she is, where she comes from, or how a crow learned how to speak in the first place. I should probably ask about that last part first, that has really been bugging me. "Hey Shadow."

"Yes." Her voice has suddenly become serious, noticing how uncomfortable I am. I fall silent for a moment, unsure of how to ask her all of these personal questions.

"Shadow, how-"

"Come on Tigre, it's time to go." My Uncle Diego calls from outside my door. I hear him walk toward the exit and Shadow shrugs her wings at me.

"It's okay. You can ask me about it later." Shadow flies off my dresser and straight into the Crow Medal on my chest. I take off the medal so that nobody will see it and ask questions about it. I place it in my pocket so that I still have it with me. Taking one last look in the mirror, I head out the door and get into my uncle's car. Putting my seatbelt on, I can see from the corner of my eye that my uncle is smiling. Him smiling isn't something unusual, but this smile looks as if he is at the happy level of winning the lottery.

"What are you so happy about?" I ask, a

little nervous about the answer.

"I'm just glad that I'm finally able to meet Colomba. You've been talking about her practically every day since you started high school." My stomach suddenly feels as if it is full of creepy, crawly things.

"Please don't embarrass me in front of her and her family. I haven't met any member of her family yet and I want to make a good impression." Uncle Diego just chuckles at me.

"Don't worry, I'll be there for just a moment and then I'll be gone. I just want to meet her, that's all." I lower my head feeling a bit guilty for what I said.

"I'm sorry. I just don't want any of them to think badly of me." Uncle Diego surprises me by chuckling again.

"It's alright. Your father acted the same way when he first started dating your mother. No matter what, everything had to be perfect. You remind me so much of him sometimes." He falls silent as a mournful expression crosses his face. This always happens whenever he talks about my parents. Even though they both died many years ago, he still feels pain whenever he talks about them. I was so young when they died that I don't even remember them. If the thought of them though can still make my uncle sad so many years later, I know that they must have been really good people.

We drive for a few more minutes in silence before we finally turn into the driveway of Colomba's house. It is a long driveway that turns and hides her house in a clump of trees, so I have never been able to see what Colomba's house looks like even though the bus would always drop her off at the end of her driveway every day. When I do see it though, I am not surprised that Colomba lives in such a beautiful house.

The house is old, but very well taken care of. It almost looks like a cottage you would see in a book of fairytales. It is made of dark stones that are almost completely covered by vines of flowers that climb up it. Tulips grow along the front of the house in neat little flowerbeds. In the front yard is a large tree that has a small swing made from rope and a small piece of wood that gently swings in the breeze.

When you look at the place you automatically just feel calmer. As if this is a place of peace, where nothing bad has ever happened. It may not be a large or fancy place, but it has a simple beauty about it that makes it seem perfect.

My uncle parks the car and I take in a deep breath before I get out and walk up to the front door with my uncle beside me. I head to the door with my extra-large sketchbook and pencils in my hands. I take in another deep breath before I knock on the door. It doesn't take long for a man, who appears to be in his late forties or early fifties, to answer the door with a smile on his face. He is a few inches shorter than me, which helps me see quite clearly that his dark hair is thinning out on top. His blue eyes look at me with friendliness.

"You must be Luis. It's a pleasure to finally meet you. I am Colomba's father." He holds out his hand for me to shake, which I accept with a nervously shaky hand. I think he noticed since I see him smile a little bit. Stupid, stupid, stupid.

"It's a pleasure to meet you too Sir."

"Come on in. Colomba is in the kitchen." He lets me and Uncle Diego in and the three of us enter a very cozy living room. A small fireplace is on one wall with a couch on the opposite wall. A small chest acts as a coffee table in front of that couch. The chest is currently open, revealing board games and other fun objects inside. Colomba has told us that she and her grandmother do a lot of needlework together, and that is clearly displayed in this room. I can see a few handmade quilts and blankets sitting in a basket beside the couch while a few cross stitch and embroidery projects are displayed in frames on the wall.

One of the embroidery pieces catches my eye though. It is hanging on the wall beside the couch. A white piece of fabric has, what looks like, a dove and a crow flying together, holding a piece of pink ribbon between them in their beaks. Beneath the two birds are two sets of initials and a date, but I am too far away to clearly see what it says. I want to take a closer look at it, but Colomba's father leads me and my uncle into the kitchen and I follow eagerly behind. The strange needlework quickly forgotten.

The three of us enter the kitchen to find Colomba and a much older woman standing in front of the sink washing dishes. The two of them laugh together as the older woman playfully flicks some water onto Colomba's face. They both smile at us when they finally notice that they are no longer alone.

"Hi Luis, glad you could come." Some soap suds are on her cheek, she looks so adorable.

"Glad to be here." Her grandmother tells her that she will finish up the dishes so that we can get started on the drawing. The two of us head out the back door and into her backyard. I look around the yard, impressed by the beauty of it. The yard is contained within a short stone wall that seems to be made of the same kind of stones as the house. In the back corner of the walled in portion of the backyard is a vegetable garden that is well tended and producing many vegetables. A large apple tree is in the opposite corner of the yard which creates shade over most of the yard while many flowers grow in the dirt around the tree. A small pond sits in the center where I can see a few fish swimming within it. Colomba was right, this is good scenery for a portrait.

"Where would you like me to be?" Colomba asks with an eager smile. I quickly glance around the yard, trying to find the perfect spot. I point beneath the apple tree.

"How about there with all the flowers behind you?" She walks over to it with me following behind. "Okay. Try sitting on that protruding root and look over toward me." She does what I ask.

"How is this?" She asks as she adjusts herself on the tree root. Her white dress modestly covers her legs a few inches past the knees. A dark blue ribbon wraps around her waist and is tied in a bow at her back. She looks so cute.

"You look perfect." I notice a faint blush form on her cheeks when I compliment her. I will need to make sure that, when I am coloring in the portrait, I include the blush. It makes her look beautiful. "Now just keep that position and I'll get started." I back up a little bit and lean against the back wall. Setting my box of pencils down on top of the wall, I grab a pencil from inside and open up my extra-large sketchbook to the first blank page and begin the portrait.

I start working on her face first since I know that this is the most important part of the portrait. A portrait is made to display a person, so the face is kind of the centerpiece of a portrait. I pay careful attention to the eyes, since I think that is her most captivating feature. The first few minutes pass by in silence before we both start chatting. Colomba has a hard time not breaking out into a smile or laughing while we talk since she needs to hold still for the portrait.

Time seems to pass so quickly as we talk. I'm almost surprised that when I look up into the sky the sun is already in the middle of the sky. Signaling that it is now midday. Wow. I've been here half the day and it barely feels as if an hour has passed. A sudden sound catches my attention. I glance around to see that the older woman who had been washing dishes with Colomba earlier has just come out the back door.

"If you children are willing to take a break, I've made some lunch for you." Colomba turns to smile at her.

"Thank you Nonna. We will be in in a

moment." She smiles sweetly to me. "Ready?"

"In just a moment." I make one last finishing touch to some of the flowers around the apple tree and I am done with the initial drawing. I look down at it with pride. It looks perfect. All I have to do now is color it in and I will be finished. I pack up my stuff and bring it with me as Colomba and I walk inside. We both enjoy a lunch of sandwiches and fruit salad before we head back out and finish the portrait. By the time we are through the sun is just beginning to set. My uncle picks me up not too long after that to bring me home. As I sit in the car, I stare at the portrait I did, feeling proud that I could create something like this. I have only been able to feel true pride in anything only a few times in my life. Almost all of those times involved art. I'm just glad that this moment included Colomba.

# Chapter Five
## Colomba-
## Shay

Everyone is bustling around me as they get everything ready for the contests for the fair. I am on the fairgrounds now in the tent where all the contests will be taking place. My grandmother is currently filling out the papers required to take part in the contests while I am looking around. I am glancing through the art section for the contests and I feel my stomach churn a little bit. Luis told me yesterday when he came to my house that he would be turning his stuff in later in the day, so I don't see anything of his lined up with the other artworks. What is making me feel a little uneasy is how good some of the other artwork is.

I walk past tables that have various artworks displayed on it. Most of them look professional. Multiple styles of art line across the tables from paintings, drawings, sculptures, pottery, and even a statue made out of bottle caps. I have no idea how that weird statue can be considered art though since it doesn't really look like anything except a giant mass of bottle caps, and it is super ugly, but I guess if they thought it was good enough to put in a contest then I shouldn't judge.

Should I have convinced Luis to join these competitions? Have I only led him here just to get his heart broken? Luis is a very shy guy; I've known this ever since I met him. It has been only within the past few months that I have seen him get more confident. If he fails in this will he go back to how he was before? Art is one of the few things that Luis feels confident about. If he loses these contests, will he lose that confidence? No, no, no, Luis is a great artist, I know this. He still has a chance to win something. It may not be first place, but maybe he'll get second or third. You still get a ribbon for that so it's not that bad. I hope that Luis can win first place, but when I look at all the other beautiful artworks around me, I lose some of my hope in that.

I had so much fun working with Luis the other day. It was a bit exhausting to hold that same position for so long, but Luis would give me little breaks to stretch and everything, so that made it better. He showed it to me afterward, it was beautiful. I'm afraid he made me look far more attractive than I actually am, but I was flattered nonetheless.

I was a bit worried when he walked in the door that he might have seen a needlework piece that my grandmother did ages ago. My grandmother was the Silver Dove before me, and my grandfather was the Crow before this new one. When they got married, my grandmother did a piece of embroidery to commemorate the day. She made one with a crow and a dove holding a pink ribbon between their two beaks. Beneath that it has their initials for their names, Sera Destephono and Giovanni Catania, and their wedding date. I forgot to put that down. I thought that if he saw that then he might put two and two together to realize that my family might have a connection with the Crow and Silver Dove. Thankfully, he didn't see it. Either that or he did see it and didn't think anything of it. I'm happy with either of those two options.

On the other side of the room I see someone familiar to me, Rosie. She is apparently entering some of her plants into the gardening competitions judging from the potted plants that she is dragging behind her in a little wagon. Several months ago, she was transformed by the Crow to become the Black Iris, with the power of having complete control over plants. She was getting bullied because she is autistic, so the Crow decided to "make things better" for her by giving her those powers and I had to step in as Silver Dove to stop him.

Rosie notices me looking at her and gives me a shy but knowing smile. I return the smile and give her a nod of greeting. She always has that knowing look in her eyes whenever she sees me, and I know why. She is the only person to have ever figured out who I really am. She knows that I am Silver Dove. I am not afraid about this though. I know that she will keep my secret. I am her friend and I have helped her, so she will repay me by keeping my secret.

I walk out of the art section to find myself standing near the table for the beauty contest my grandmother had told me about the other day. All around the table are girls close to my own age. They are all talking and giggling excitedly with each other as they fill out the paperwork to enter the contest at a few small tables they have set up for people to write on. I almost walked right past the contest table without a second look, but then I see a girl at the table and the sight of her makes me stop.

The girl standing in the front of the table for the beauty contest has to be one of the most beautiful girls I have ever seen. Her tanned skin is the color of light caramel, making the brightness of her soft blue eyes stand out even more. Her hair falls down her back in gentle curls that are the color of wheat. She is a few inches taller than me and has the body of those women you see in fashion magazines. Just from looking at this girl I know who she is even though we have never met. Her name is Shay and she is a year or two older than me. Even though she technically lives here in this town, she is barely ever here. She is a model, so she is always going to places like New York, Chicago, or San Francisco to do photo shoots and other stuff like that. Since she is always going from one place to another she does her schooling online. I suppose she is having a little break from her modeling since she appears to be signing up for the beauty contest.

As soon as she has been given her paperwork to sign up for the contest, she turns around to look for a table that she can write on. When she gets close to some of the tables that some of the other girls are writing on, they turn to glare at her, clearly showing that she is not welcome. She leaves them behind and comes over to the table that I am standing next to.

"Do you mind if I stand here?" She has a voice to match her appearance. A beautiful voice that is soft and sweet.

"I don't mind. I'm not using the table." She looks surprised.

"Are you not signing up for the contest?" I shake my head.

"No, I'm not. I'm here with my grandmother to sign up for some of the other contests. We do a lot of baking and needlework." She smiles sweetly to me.

"Oh, that's too bad. You are so adorable. I'm sure you could win." I know that if she's in the contest, I would definitely not win.

"Thanks, but I'm already in so many other contests that this would be kind of overkill." She nods at that, understanding what I mean.

"Well, I hope you and your grandmother win a few ribbons. My name is Shay by the way." She extends her hand out to me which I gladly shake.

"I'm Colomba, it's a pleasure to meet you. I hope you win in your contest as well." From the other side of the tent I can hear my grandmother calling my name. "Oh, that's my grandmother. I have to go. Have a good day." She waves goodbye to me as I make my way through the crowd to get to my grandmother. When I look at the other girls though, judging from the cold glares that they are directing at Shay, I don't think that they are hoping that she wins like I do. It looks more like they hope that she will throw away her entry papers and get out so that they never have to see her again. When I look at them glaring at her, I silently pray that Shay will be alright.

# Chapter Six
## Luis-
## The Fortune
## Teller

As I pass through the front entrance of the fairgrounds, I am completely in awe by what I see. My eyes scan everything around me, absolutely fascinated by all the activity around me. People are moving in every direction, trying to get things set up for when the fair opens tomorrow. A tent slowly rises beside me as several men pull on some ropes and tie them down to prevent the tent from falling. People shuffle about from here to there as they carry random things or bark out orders to other people. I hold my artwork close to me to make sure that nobody accidently knocks it out of my hands in all this activity.

I have gone to the county fair only a few times in my life, back when I was a lot younger. I went then because I was a kid and my uncle took me. At that age it is still considered alright to have a father figure take you to the fair, but when you get older it makes you look like a loser. People already think

I'm a loser. If I went with my uncle or by myself, I would look even more like a loser, so I decided to just stay home after that. I forgot how amazing a fair can look.

I have three drawings with me now; one of a crow and another that I did of a tree with a crow flying above it, both drawings that I did for art class, as well as the portrait I did yesterday. I really wanted to enter the competition for song writing that I had seen the other day at the diner, but I didn't finish the one I was working on. Oh well, I can live with that. The only reason I didn't finish was because I spent all my time working on the portrait. I am very proud of the portrait I did so I shouldn't be disappointed that I spent so much time on it.

As I pass by a few tents that are getting set up with either games or items for people to buy inside, I think I hear someone say my name. My eyes lead my gaze to a tent that is made of brightly colored fabric in designs so strange that I don't think I could ever explain it in words. The tent is mainly dark purple with designs in gold, black, and red. When I look at it, it almost reminds me of designs I had seen on gypsy clothing from old movies that my uncle and I watch together. The piece of fabric acting as the door is being held open by a small, delicate looking hand, while the other hand is beckoning me inside. My curiosity overcomes my discomfort and I walk toward the strange tent.

I enter the strange looking tent to see a woman who looks as if she is in her early twenties sitting on the ground in front of a low table. She is a pretty woman wrapped in an unusual, robe like garment with a hood that she has down made of black fabric printed with strange designs. Her short dark hair, almost the same length as most men's, is pulled back by an intricately patterned black scarf. Her eyes are so dark that they are almost black. There is a calm intelligence in those eyes. It's almost as if she holds all the secrets of the world. A single earring hangs from one ear, a small golden chain with what looks like the fang of a predator hanging from it, maybe a wolf's tooth. She smiles at me slyly, as if she already knows everything about me just from taking one look at me.

"Come in young man. You have a lot that you want to know, don't you?" I slowly walk closer to the woman, feeling a little uneasy. It's something about her eyes that makes me feel this way. It's almost as if she is looking straight through me and into my soul.

Sitting down in front of her little table across from her, I look down at the various items on the table. A crystal ball, fortune telling cards, a bowl with strange herbs and other items are sitting beside it waiting to be mixed together, and some things that I have never seen before and couldn't even guess as to what they're used for. She smiles at me as I stare at her strange objects.

"Do not worry, I never use those. I just keep them there to add an air of mystery in the room since that is what people expect from a fortune teller. Those are items that are used to trick people, nothing more. For me to see and understand what the future holds for you, I merely need to look into your eyes. Can you look into my eyes for a moment?" I shyly lift my eyes to look into hers, but as soon as our eyes meet it feels as if I am trapped by her gaze. I don't think I could look away even if I wanted to. It feels like an eternity passes before she tears her gaze away from mine and I have to hold back a sigh of relief.

"There is a lot that I see in you, young man. You are in a lot of pain." I look back up at her in surprise. What did she just say? "You constantly feel as if you are fighting just to make it through each day. People hurt you constantly even though you have done nothing to them. I can assure you though that this will change for you. One day, you will have peace." I lean in closer, completely absorbed by what she has said.

"What else did you see?" She smiles at me softly, amused by my sudden interest.

"I can easily see that you are in love with a girl." I look away from her again, suddenly uncomfortable. "You are good friends with her, but she doesn't realize how you feel about her. You want to tell her, but you are afraid. There is no need for your fear. Tell her how you feel. You two are meant to be together. You will one day be with the girl of your dreams." I smile at the woman in front of me, feeling as if a huge weight has been taken off my chest. I don't believe in fortune telling, but for some reason this seemed real to me.

"Thank you very much, how much do I owe you for the fortune?" She shakes her head at me with a smile.

"You do not have to pay. This was just for your benefit." The two of us stand up and she leads me back outside her tent.

"Thank you so much for everything. You have a good day Ma'am." I start walking away and I hear her saying something from behind me.

"You do not have to call me Ma'am. My real name is Corva, but most people have known me as Shadow." I feel my eyes grow wide as I quickly turn around, but the young woman is no longer there. I run back to the tent, but when I look inside the woman isn't there either. There isn't even any evidence that she was there. The little table that had all the fortune telling stuff is gone and has been replaced by a much larger table covered in homemade candles that a lady is setting up to try and sell at the fair.

I walk out of the tent feeling very confused as I head toward the tent where I will enter my drawings and sketches in the art competition. Swallowing back all of my fear, I hold my folder full of drawings close to my chest. They are my shield to the world. I hold my shield close to me as I enter the competition tent, getting ready to give them my shield to judge. Getting ready to give them what feels like a piece of my soul.

When I am inside the tent, I am surprised by how much activity is going on inside. People are bustling all over the place, talking to workers there to have their stuff entered in the contests or talking with each other, comparing their work to other people's. I can feel my shoulders closing in toward my body and my head lowering in my fear of what is going on. I am walking through the art section of the contests now and I am looking at the other people's work. It all looks so professional while my stuff is only the work of a kid who has no professional experience whatsoever. I am starting to regret even thinking about entering these contests. All of the other artists here are far older than me, and probably have a lot more experience in the art world too. I just draw a bunch of pictures in my high school art class. Why did I even think about doing this? I'm such an idiot.

I'm about to walk out of the tent when I am stopped by an older woman who, apparently, is helping out with setting up the contests based on the T-shirt she is wearing that is bright yellow and only says the word, Worker.

"Hello young man. Are you here to enter one of the contests?" I lower my eyes from hers, staring down at the drawings in my hands. There's no turning back now.

"Yes, yes I am. I'm here to enter some drawings into the… the uh,… the competitions for the drawings of animals, landscapes, and the portraits." I glance up to see that the woman is smiling at me with true friendliness.

"That's wonderful, I'm so excited for you. Now, just come right over here and I will get you signed up. We can get everything done in a flash." I give her my drawings and she hands me a few papers to fill out with my personal information as well as the information on my drawings. It only takes me and the woman a few minutes to fill everything out and then I am on my way back home with empty hands, but a stomach full of butterflies as I try to think about why I got myself into this mess.

# <u>Chapter Seven</u>
## Colomba-
## The Fair

$A$ huge smile is on my face as I stare at everything around me. The rides whirl around and dip close to the ground before quickly rising back up so that the people riding it scream with both terror and delight. Children run through the crowd to try and make it to the rides faster than their friends while their parents watch over them. The bright, colorful lights dazzle my eyes as I walk through a cleared path with tents on either side displaying either items to sell or games to play. The air is full of the scents of sugary, fried fair foods. The area seems to buzz with cheerful noises with the children laughing, popcorn popping, and the rides with the people on them roaring and screaming.

I rush through all the joyful chaos to head toward the Ferris Wheel. Luis and I decided to meet there so that we could have some fun together. Nat isn't able to come today since she and her parents are celebrating her grandfather's birthday in his home in a neighboring town, but she should be able to come with us in the following days of the fair. Nat and I have always gone to the fairs together each and every year. It's one of our favorite things to do. I have so many fond memories of us playing the fair games and eating so much junk food that we both got sick on one of the rides. Even though we both threw up, we still had a good time. I hope that we can create just as many beautiful memories with Luis now that he is part of our little group of friends.

Out of all the rides here the Ferris Wheel is the tallest of them all, so I easily find my way toward it. When I make it there, I feel almost like an ant because of how small I am compared to that thing. Compared to the other rides, the line for the Ferris Wheel is the shortest. This is probably because everybody wants to go on the fast, exciting rides, while the Ferris Wheel just looks kind of tame when you look at everything else.

It doesn't take long for Luis to show up and we start wandering through the fair to look at all the tents with games or stuff for people to sell. We both thought it would be a good idea to wait to go on all the rides until a little later when all the little kids have gone home, that way the lines will be shorter.

The two of us chat as we look through tent after tent, looking at all the beautiful, as well as strange, things people are selling. The two of us got a good chuckle looking through a guy's tent who was selling pigs that he had dressed up in costumes. Neither of us have any idea why he decided to dress up those pigs, but it was sure hilarious to look at. My particular favorite was a pig dressed as a princess, complete with a little tiara and frilly, pink dress.

We were about to pass by one tent that was selling jewelry without even looking inside, but something catches my eye and I stop. I look down at the display of jewelry, captivated by the beautiful necklaces. One of them really grabs my attention, one set on display on the neck of a bust of a woman's head. It has a plain silver chain with a small glass pendant hanging at the bottom that's in the shape of an orb. Within the orb is colored glass that's shaped like a blue flower. It is a simple necklace, but a beautiful one.

"You like that one, don't you?" Luis looks at the necklace I had been admiring. I lower my eyes, a little embarrassed that I had been admiring it so obviously.

"Yeah, it's really beautiful." I glance at the price tag on it. "I would get it, but my grandmother and I are saving up to get a new sewing machine. The one we have now is acting all weird. I tried to sew two pieces of fabric together the other day, I thought that thing was going to eat the fabric." I turn away from the necklace, not wanting to look at what I can't have. "I can get something like that another day, now come on let's go have some fun." I take his hand and lead him away to head to the other side of the fair where all of the rides are. It hurts a little knowing that I can't afford something that I really want, but there are more important things in life than pretty jewelry.

My grandmother and I both agreed to put our spare money into getting a new sewing machine and

I will honor that agreement. We did agree as well that I could use a couple of bucks at the fair to have some fun with my friends, but the necklace would have taken up all the money for the fair. I would rather spend the money to have fun with my friends than to blow it all on one little object. A sudden thought comes into my head, and I turn to Luis with excitement in my heart.

"How about we go into the contest tent? They're going to be starting the first round for the beauty contest today and I want to see someone I know that's in it." I want to go there and see Shay. Since she is always out of town for her modeling, I don't think she has a lot of friends here. I think she would appreciate having somebody there to wish her luck.

Luis seems a bit confused as to why I want to go there, but he doesn't argue as we start heading toward the tent. When we get inside, we are immediately caught up in a flurry of activity. Since the competition will be starting in an hour or so, everyone is busy either setting things up or the girls who are in the competition are getting prepared, putting on makeup or adjusting their dresses. Apparently this first round in the competition is some kind of formal wear thing. I'm not sure, I've never been in something like this before and I don't think I ever want to try.

I glance through the crowd to try and find Shay, but the blood freezes in my veins when I see Angela dressed in a beautiful dress, admiring herself in a mirror. Oh great, she's a part of this contest? I silently wish every girl here luck as I silently sneak past her to continue looking for Shay. Even though Luis and I search all through the tent, Shay is nowhere to be found.

"I guess she decided not to take part in the competition, let's go out the back and find something to do." Luis nods and the two of us leave out the back entrance of the tent to find the person we had been looking for. Shay is sitting on top of a wooden box with her face buried in her hands and with something colorful sitting beside her.

"Hey Shay, what's wrong? Why do you look upset?" Shay jumps a little in surprise at the sound of my voice. She calms down when she recognizes me.

"Oh hi. You're Colomba, right?" I nod my head at her. "I'm sorry, but I am upset. Someone ruined my dress." She holds up the colorful thing that had been sitting beside her to reveal a dress that had been slashed across the front, making it unwearable.

"Who did this?" Shay tosses the dress back down on the box.

"I don't know. They just left this for me, I found it pinned to my ruined dress." She holds out a piece of paper to me that I take and read. The words on it break my heart.

**Get out of this contest now or it will get worse.**

"Is there anything we can do to find this person?" Shay shakes her head.

"No. I already asked everybody, and they all said that they didn't see anything. Either they are telling me the truth, or they are covering for the person who did this. The competition starts in an hour and I have nothing to wear. I'm going to have to quit before it even starts." I surprise her by smiling.

"No, you don't. I can fix this for you no problem." Opening up my purse, I pull out a little sewing kit that I always carry with me. I take the ruined dress and start threading one of my needles when I hear Luis chuckle behind me.

"Why am I not surprised that you carry around a sewing kit?" I smirk back at him as I start to fix the dress.

"You're not surprised because you know that I am awesome." That actually gets Shay to smile, and we all stay silent as I quickly sew together the ripped fabric. It takes about twenty minutes, but I finish it.

Shay and I leave Luis outside so that we can go inside to try on the dress and make sure it fits correctly. As soon as we find an empty changing room, she slips off her clothes and puts on the dress. I help zip her up and then examine the dress to find that it looks better than I thought it would. You can't even tell that it had been ripped in the first place. It is a pink gown that goes almost all the way to the ground. It is strapless and has a layer of lace that acts as a second layer on top. The bottom layer is of a shimmery dark pink, while the lace on top is a pretty, bright pink. Some of that same shimmery, dark pink material is used on top to act almost like a belt around her waist. Because of the tear in the lace, I had to take some of the lace off and I used that bits of lace to turn it into a flower that I sewed on the side of her waist on the little belt. I'm pretty impressed with myself that I could do something like this in just a couple minutes.

"What do you think, Shay?" She is smiling at herself in the mirror, hope lighting up her eyes.

"It's perfect. Thank you so much." She wraps her arms around me in a tight hug that I return. "I've got to go get everything else ready before we start, but can you please stay and watch the competition? It would mean a lot to me."

"Of course, I will. Now you go ahead and get ready. I'm going to go get Luis and we will find a seat." She runs off with an excited smile while I head to the back exit to find Luis.

# Chapter Eight
## Luis-
## Cheating

Colomba and Shay run inside the contest tent to try on the dress Colomba just fixed, leaving me alone outside. I was about to sit down on the wooden box Shay had been sitting on moments before, but I hear a familiar voice and I start walking toward it to the other side of the tent. When I make it to the corner of the tent, I stay there to make sure that they don't see me. I peek one eye around the corner to see the principal of my school, who is also the mayor of this town and Angela's father, talking with the one of the judges for the beauty contest that I had seen earlier when Colomba and I were walking through the tent searching for Shay.

Angela's father is a rather tall man with hair that is almost completely grey. My guess is that he used to be a very handsome man in his youth, but he looks a bit tired and stressed. I would be too if I raised Angela. Every time I have ever seen him, he is wearing a suit and it is always perfectly pressed and clean. He looks like the perfect picture of a small-town politician. He always looks his best and has a nearly constant smile on his face. That smile is not there at the moment though.

He and the judge are talking very closely, well I can't really say that they are talking, it looks far more serious than a pleasant little chat. Angela's dad is standing close to the judge, as if they are talking about something secret.

"Now listen to me George," Angela's father growls to the judge, "You can take this money with no questions asked and my little girl wins this silly contest. There isn't anything wrong with that, it's not like it's a scholarship for college or anything. It's just a stupid beauty contest, and I know that my little girl wants to win it. She deserves it too. She's always been such a pretty girl; you know that she should win this." The judge, who is apparently named George, scratches the back of his head. He looks pretty uncomfortable with what is going on right now, but he looks tempted to take the little bundle of money that Angela's dad is holding out to him.

"I'm not sure Larry, this doesn't seem right." Angela's dad's already menacing face seems to get even more intimidating.

"I know what you're thinking George. You want to give the prize to that Shay kid. It wouldn't be fair to everyone else George. She's a professional model. It was unfair to even have her enter this contest. Let the other girls have a chance, especially the one girl who really deserves it." Angela's dad holds the money closer to the judge, who takes it with a small smile playing at the corner of his lips.

"Alright Larry, I'll do my best." I quickly run back to where Shay and Colomba had left me. As soon as I get there, I look over my shoulder to make sure that they didn't hear me and come after me.

I can't believe what I just saw. The mayor of our town is bribing a judge to make his daughter the winner of a beauty contest? What is up with that? This is messed up. How can our own mayor, and the principal of my school, do something like that? Why couldn't those two men see that this is wrong? Am I the only one that sees how terrible this is? I know that this is just a simple county fair contest, but a lot of the girls in that tent looked very excited about it. It would be terrible to know that they all lost because of some selfish bribery.

Colomba comes out a few moments later, ready to bring me inside the tent again so that we can watch the event and cheer Shay on. I don't say a word about what I saw to her, or to anyone. I don't think anybody would believe me if I told them about what the mayor and judge did. I don't think that they would want to believe me.

The two of us sit in the third row and chat while we wait for the show to begin. It doesn't take long for the lights to dim, signaling the start of the competition. One of the judges comes out and does some announcing and whatever, I don't really pay attention. I only focus on what's happening on the stage when Shay steps on. She does look very nice in the dress Colomba fixed up. I know that she's a model and everything, but I still think that Colomba is prettier. Some people may not agree with me, but that's what I think. Shay appeared very modest and sweet, but when Angela came on the stage right after she was a far cry from modest and sweet. She struts onto the stage in a dress that practically anybody would consider inappropriate. She is walking as if she owns the room and everyone in it. Wow, how could anybody look so stuck up? I have to keep myself from laughing at how snotty she looks.

After all the contestants have walked around the stage in their formal dresses, the judges go off to a separate room to make their decisions on the winners. Why is this an actual contest? I mean they didn't even really do anything, they just walked around the stage in pretty dresses. It's not like they did anything spectacular. It also seems pretty insulting to the girls taking part in the contest. They are just paraded around like show dogs instead of actual people. I am so confused, but I'm not going to say anything about it.

A few minutes pass before the judges return to their judging table while the entire room grows silent. One of them stands up, telling all the contests that they all did a wonderful job and blah, blah, blah, blablah; but then he finally says that they have decided on a winner. Most of the audience members seem to lean in closer to him in their excitement. I am entirely shocked when he says that Shay is the winner while Angela only gets second place in this part of the competition. The man states that the next part of the competition will take part at the same time and place tomorrow afternoon before the crowd starts to get up and comfort the girls in the contest who didn't win. Shay stands all alone with nobody to congratulate her. Most of the people give her dirty looks as they pass her, as if she is to blame for why their girl lost. Colomba and I go over to her to congratulate her.

While she and Shay chat, I glance over to see Angela's dad glaring at the judge he had bribed earlier while the judge tries to look anywhere but near Angela's dad. I guess that Angela's dad wasn't able to bribe all the judges and the one he did bribe wasn't able to convince the other two judges to vote for Angela. The best he was able to do was to give her second place.

I try to forget about all that though as I join in Shay and Colomba's conversation again. It only lasts for another few minutes before Shay goes off to get changed out of her nice dress while Colomba and I go out to enjoy the rest of the fair before her father and my uncle come to pick us up. The two of us go on almost every ride before the sun has completely disappeared and we walk to the exit to get picked up. It doesn't take long for my uncle to show up and he takes me home. When I am alone in my room, I place my hand on top of my Crow Medal and Shadow appears on my windowsill.

"Good evening Master."

"Hey Shadow, what do you think I should do about what I saw with the mayor and the judge?" She chuckles.

"I think you should do the obvious. Do what you think is right." I look away from her, shaking my head.

"I know, but can you tell me what the right

thing is? I mean, I know that nobody would believe me if I told them that the mayor is bribing the judge. Who would believe a teenage loser like me?" She flies off the windowsill to land on the dresser in front of me so that we are looking at each other eye to eye.

"I would believe you, your uncle would believe you, your art teacher, Mr. Sizemore, would believe you, and Colomba would believe you. Just because you think so badly of yourself doesn't mean that your words aren't valuable." I turn away from her again.

"They might, but nobody that's important for this contest would believe me. They would think that I'm lying so that one of the contests would look bad. There must be another way of dealing with this. Shay seems really nice, and if this contest were fair I know that she would win."

"I know that you will come up with the right thing to do. You are an intelligent young man who has already figured out the solutions to much more difficult questions." I smile at her.

"Thank you, Shadow. You always seem to know how to make me feel better." I pause for a moment, a little uncomfortable with what I feel needs to be said. "Hey Shadow."

"Yes, Master?" She looks at me curiously, wondering why I suddenly sound so serious again.

"When I was turning stuff in for the contests at the fair, I met someone there. A fortune teller told me that people call her Shadow. She seemed to know a lot about me. Did… do you know anything about that?" Shadow cocks her head to the side in confusion.

"Are you trying to ask me if I was that person just because we have the same name?" I can feel myself blushing because I know how stupid it must sound to her. It sounds pretty stupid to me and I'm the one that said it. Even though I am very embarrassed, I still nod my head yes. "Fortune tellers know how to play with your mind. They tell you very vague things that most people would associate with themselves. Just because she said something that sounds like something from your life doesn't mean that she knows you. Also, many people have probably used the name Shadow before to sound more mysterious. Just because something seems to be connected doesn't mean that it is." I lower my head as I smile to myself. Well I feel like an idiot.

"I'm sorry Shadow. I shouldn't have asked you something so ridiculous."

"It's alright Master, we all make mistakes." Without another word she flies off of my dresser and flies straight into the medal where she immediately disappears. When I look at the clock, I realize how late it is, so I get ready for bed. Once I am in my pajamas I get under my blankets and close my eyes to go to sleep. I feel as if I am about to fall asleep when my eyes pop open as a sudden realization comes over me.

Shadow never really answered the question. She never said yes or no to whether or not she was the woman I met at the fair. She danced around the question, and I don't think she will ever give me a straight answer. I stay up for another hour thinking about this before I realize that I will never understand what really happened there. I will just have to live with the uncertainty.

# Chapter Nine
## Colomba-
## Peanut Butter

I walk through the fair alone for now. This is the second day of the fair, as well as the second day of competing for the beauty contest that I am heading to now. Luis and Nat said that they couldn't get here until a bit later so I'm going over to see how Shay is doing. I want to make sure that nobody else is messing with her. When that mysterious person wrecked her dress, they warned her that it would get worse if she stayed in the contest. She has stayed and has won the first event. Whoever it was who left that note won't be very happy about that.

I enter the contest tent to find a very strange scene happening inside. Shay is standing in front of a mirror examining something strange hidden within her blonde curls. A pink blob is now stuck in her hair, bubble gum. Oh jeez, I know the pain of having bubble gum stuck in your hair. It is not pleasant, but I know how to get rid of it.

"Hey Shay, what happened here?" She jumps a little as she tears her gaze away from her reflection to look at me in surprise.

"Oh Colomba, I didn't hear you coming up. I accidently got some gum stuck in my hair. Isn't that ridiculous?" Something about the tone of her voice doesn't sound right to me. It almost sounds as if she is close to tears. Is she telling me the truth here?

"C'mon, I know how we can get it out. Follow me and I can help you." I take her hand and lead her out of the tent toward a large building that I know is currently empty. I pull out some keys from my purse to open one of the doors.

"My church uses this building for a lot of events. They gave me a key for it since I do a lot of the setting up for the events. What we need should be in here." I take her inside to a small kitchen. I look through a few of the cabinets along the walls before I finally find what I am looking for.

"Here we are. I hope you're not allergic to this." I hold up a jar of peanut butter, which Shay looks at with confusion.

"Peanut butter?"

"Yeah, you use this to help get gum out of your hair. It may take a few minutes to do, but it's better than chopping your hair off." I have Shay sit down on a stool while I open up the jar. "I'm just going to take some of this peanut butter and put it in your hair, around where the gum is. That will loosen up the gum so that it will come off. My grandmother had to do this to me when I was six and I was trying to blow a bubble with the gum, and it popped all over my face and into my hair." I dip my fingers into the peanut butter and I gently start using it on her hair. As my peanut butter covered fingers work through the gum in her hair, I notice the tears beginning to glide down her face.

"What's wrong Shay?" She lets out a faint sob before her broken voice gives me the heart-breaking answer.

"I'm sorry, I lied to you. This wasn't an accident. One of the other girls who is in the contest stuck her gum in my hair. She said that I didn't deserve to win. She said that since I'm already a model I should just quit, that I shouldn't be such a showoff. I don't really want to be in this contest, but I need the money so that I can go to college." She buries her face in her hands as she breaks down and sobs. "Nobody ever believes me when I say that. They think that just because I'm pretty I don't have a brain in my head! I want to go to school so I can become an engineer, but I don't have the money to do that. I never wanted to get into modeling and all that, but it is a good job, so I took it. I didn't want to do this contest, but my manager told me that we wouldn't have any photo shoots for a while. Because of that, I needed to find a quick way to make some money while I was home. I saw the ad for the contest and saw that it had a cash prize, so I decided to try. I only have one year left before I graduate from high school and I want to go to college right after that. I don't have all the time in the world to get the money I'll need." She laughs pitifully through her tears. "To think, I thought that this was going to be fun, but no. Everyone in the contest is treating me like I'm a terrible person just because I'm pretty. I don't understand this at all! Why do they hate me so much? They don't even know me." As I continue to slowly get the peanut butter out of her hair, I think about what she just said. That is very true. Most people don't really expect a pretty girl to be intelligent. It is a sad thing to think about, but it is true. When I look at the girl in front of me, I think I understand why the other girls are making fun of her and I try to explain it to her in the gentlest way I can.

"I don't think that they really hate you." She lifts her tear streaked face from her hands to look at me with confusion. "They hate that you are considered prettier than them. Ever since a girl is born, she is constantly told that she has to be pretty. Most of the time it's done in a subtle way. All of the female heroes in stories are pretty while most of the female villains are ugly. The pretty girls always get more attention. And the girls who are considered less attractive are teased because they don't look the way that the world tells them they should. When a girl sees another girl who is prettier than them, they feel threatened. They don't want to have the competition. They will do what they can to make the other girl go away or feel bad about themselves. For you, that means that they tease you and put gum in your hair." She looks back down as I continue to work the gum out of her hair.

"What should I do? How can I live through this?" This time I am the one that looks down. "They have been putting terrible lies about me all over A-Streamer. It's as if they are all trying their best to make me look like the worst. What am I going to do?" I know that this isn't what she wants to hear, but if I am going to be honest with her then

I need to tell her this.

"I don't know. I have never lived through something like this. If I was in your place, if I saw who was doing this to me, I would tell one of the people in charge so that they could deal with them. I would just keep going, showing them that they cannot hurt me. You are the one who gets to decide whether or not what they do hurts your feelings. You are in charge of your own emotions."

The two of us stay in silence while I work the rest of the gum out of her hair. It takes around fifteen minutes to work it all out and then wash the peanut butter from her hair. After that is all through, I take her back to the competition tent so that she can start getting ready while I head outside to meet up with Nat and Luis. Once we have found each other, we play a few games and ride some of the great rides before we all head to the competition tent to watch Shay. With what she is going through right now, she needs all the support she can get.

# <u>Chapter Ten</u>
## Luis-
## The Right
## Decision

I am wandering around the fair now, keeping my eyes open for Colomba. I told her that I would be arriving late, but that is a lie. I told her that I wasn't going to be here until about an hour from now, so I need to make sure that she doesn't see me before I get my business done. I thought long and hard about what I saw yesterday with Angela's dad and the judge, and I also thought about what Shadow said to me. She was right, I am smart enough to come up with a way to fix this problem. I know this because I have found a way to fix the problem.

Sneaking into the competition tent, I let myself kind of blend into the background. Nobody really seems to notice me as I quietly observe everyone, trying to find a specific person. It doesn't take long to spot him, the judge that Angela's dad is bribing is standing on the other side of the tent talking to the other two judges. I wait patiently until I see him end the conversation and walk away. I follow after him, making sure to be at least ten feet away from him so it doesn't really look like I'm following him. I keep my eye on him until I see him walk into a room and close the door behind him, leaving him completely alone in the room. I finally have my chance. I rush out of the tent and find a secluded spot behind some large storage boxes behind the competition tent. As fast as I can, I transform into the Crow and I send Shadow to find the judge.

Shadow flies through the air and heads straight for the room where the corrupt judge sits. She flies silently through the crowd as a shadow. Nobody sees or hears her except me. Shadow passes through the door to find the judge, she doesn't even pause for a moment before she flies straight into his heart and I speak to him in his mind.

Hello George.

The man leaps out of the chair so quickly that it topples over as he looks around the room in a panic, trying to find where the mysterious voice is coming from.

You won't find me in there George. I am the Crow and I am speaking to you through your mind.

The poor guy is practically about to wet himself he's so scared. It's kind of funny to watch. He knows who I am, he knows what I am capable of.

"What- what do you want from me?" I stay silent for a moment just to mess with him before I let out a dark chuckle in his mind, sending a shiver down his spine.

You know what my mission is George. I am here to protect the weaker people in this town, the ones who can't protect themselves. You are weak, but not the kind of person I would ever help. Despite how weak you are, you are being cruel to many girls who do not deserve it.

His mind races as he realizes that I somehow know about the bribe he took from the mayor.

Yes, I know all about that. There are many girls in this competition who are eager to win in a fair way. They can't do that if a few people are willing to cheat to get what they want. I suggest you do the right thing and return the money that was given to you and choose whoever you think is worthy of winning. If you won't do this, then we may have a problem. I would rather not speak to you again on this matter. Goodbye George.

Shadow leaves his body, but she does not leave the room. She and I both watch as the judge checks behind every large object and behind every corner to see if he can find the Crow or some prankster hidden there. When he doesn't find a soul, he knows that what happened was real and I am watching him to see if he makes the right move. He doesn't waste any time with thinking things through. He quickly pulls out his wallet and takes out a bunch of money, probably the same money that the mayor gave him the other day, and runs out the door as if he is being chased by the devil himself.

Shadow follows him closely as he makes his way into the large room where all the people involved with the contest are. He quickly finds the mayor giving his daughter endless encouragement as she gets ready for the contest, not even really paying attention to his kind words at all. The judge grabs the mayor by the shoulder with a look of terror on his face.

"Larry, you've got to come with me." The mayor looks as if he is about to tell him to back off, but when he sees the terror in the judge's eyes he agrees. The judge takes the mayor to the same spot outside the tent where he had originally taken the bribe.

"Larry- Larry I can't do it. You have to take the money back. I can't be a part of this at all." The mayor glares at the judge as if he is being betrayed by a close friend.

"What made you so spineless all of a sudden?" The judge's hands clench into fists at being called spineless, but he doesn't let his anger distract him from what needs to be done.

"Larry, the Crow talked to me. He spoke to me in my head and threatened me. He told me that if I keep the money and let you bribe me then he will do something to me. I don't know about you, but

I'm not going to keep doing this to find out what that something is." The mayor had looked annoyed and angry a few moments ago, but now he seems to share the same fear.

"Are you sure it was the Crow? Why would he get in the way of something like this?"

"I'm sure it was him. Nobody else was in the room at the time and the guy spoke in my head. He said that he was involved in this because he is the defender of the weak, or something of that sort. He wants to make sure that this competition is fair. I don't know how he knows or why he is involved, but I don't care. I don't want to have to deal with him. Just having him in my mind for two minutes was enough for me. I don't want him to do something to me just for a couple hundred bucks. Getting involved with the Crow is just not worth it." The judge places the money into the mayor's front suit pocket and turns around to head back into the tent. "You can do whatever you want, go bribe another judge, but just know that the Crow might come after you next." He walks back inside without another word, leaving the mayor behind with an expression of rage, fear, and disappointment.

Shadow returns to me and I quickly turn back into myself so that I can meet up with Colomba and Nat. When we do meet, we play a few games and ride a few rides before we go to the competition tent to see how Shay does. We arrive at just the last minute and grab a few seats near the back. The lights dim a minute later, and the second part of the competition begins.

For this part of the competition the girls are all

asked the same five questions one at a time. They are mainly just opinion questions, but the last question is what the one thing is they would wish for if they knew it would come true. I have to force myself not to roll my eyes when practically every single girl answers the final question with world peace. Oh please, I know for one thing that Angela wouldn't want that. Her number one wish would probably be to rule the world. That wouldn't surprise me in the slightest. I am delightfully surprised though when it is Shay's turn to answer the questions and when she is asked what her wish would be, she gives the greatest answer to that question I have ever heard.

"I wish that education will be praised instead of ridiculed and intelligence seen as beautiful." I am liking this Shay girl more each time I see her. Most people would never suspect that a girl as pretty as her would be very intelligent, but Shay seems to be smarter than most people I have met.

When all the girls have answered their questions, the judges went off to a separate room like before and came out a few minutes later to announce who they chose as the winner. I don't think anybody was surprised when the judges announced that they chose Shay as the winner and some girl I don't know got second place. Angela was so upset by this announcement that she stormed off the stage with her high heels stomping on the stage. Well isn't someone a drama queen? No wonder her dad's hair is nearly completely grey, I would have grey hairs too if I was the one that raised her.

The event ends and we all leave the competition tent to head back out to the fair. I glance over to the other part of the competition tent that is closed off to the public for the moment. Nobody is allowed in right now because there are judges in there right now looking over all of the stuff that people have entered into the contests to see who they pick as the winners. My stomach ties itself into knots at the thought of that. Right now, my work is being judged by complete strangers. They probably think that it's terrible. They are probably looking at my work right now, thinking that it's the pathetic work of an amateur. Why did I think I could enter my stuff in there and actually do well?

I force that thought out of my mind. I can't talk to myself like that about my artwork. Art is one of the few things in my life that I actually feel confident about, I can't let my doubt seep into that area of my life too. I have a chance. Everybody I've talked to about this thinks that I have a chance. If they believe in me then why can't I?

I turn my eyes away from that tent so that I can try to not think about any of that and enjoy my time at the fair instead. The three of us go on a few more rides before Nat says that she has to go home, leaving Colomba and I alone to hang out. I'm pretty happy about this at first, but that doesn't last long.

"Hey there you two." A voice calls out from behind us. I don't even have to turn around to know who that voice belongs to.

"Hi Alex." Colomba says with a pleasant smile on her face. Someone please kill me now. Alex comes up from behind the two of us and wraps his arms around our shoulders. For Colomba, he wraps around her gently, but for me his hand grabs onto my shoulder and I recognize the silent threat he is giving me. He is warning me not to say anything to him that will make him look bad in front of Colomba. He wants me to leave so that they can be alone. I'm afraid that I disappoint him by staying where I am.

"I was hoping that I would run into some friendly faces to play some of the games or something. You guys up for some company?" Tell him to go away, tell him to go away, tell him to go away.

"Sure, why not?" Coward. Why did I say that? Why am I asking? I know why. I don't want to look like a jerk in front of Colomba. The three of us walk together, Alex standing far too close to Colomba as we do. His eyes light up when he looks at a game next to us. It is a classic fair game where there is a long tower with a bell at the top. You are supposed to use a hammer to hit a button on the ground and that sends a little metal bar up the tower to try and ring the bell. It is a test of strength that Alex looks eager to try. Of course, a showoff like him would love a game like that.

"How about we try this one, it looks pretty fun." Colomba looks at it curiously.

"Sure, why not? I've never played this game before." I follow after the two feeling a bit uncomfortable. I've never been an athletic kind of guy. If they try and convince me to play, I know that I'm just going to embarrass myself.

Colomba gives the guy running the game the dollar she needs to play and he quickly explains how to play and tells her that if she wants to win one of the little stuffed animals he has as prizes then she will have to ring the bell. Colomba nods her head and takes the hammer in her tiny hands. The hammer is so big in her grip that it is almost funny to look at. She lifts the hammer over her shoulder and slams it down hard on the button on the ground. The little metal bar flies up the tower and misses the bell by only a few feet. Even though she didn't win, she smiles up at the tower.

"Wow! That was a lot higher than I thought it would go. Who's next?" She holds out the hammer to the two of us and Alex gives me an evil grin.

"Well how about it Louie? How about you give it a shot first?" I shake my head at him.

"No thanks, I don't want to try it." Alex chuckles at me.

"Oh, come on Louie. Don't tell me you're afraid that you're going to lose to this pretty little girl." Colomba's expression looks as if Alex just slapped her across the face. She looks so insulted by Alex's sexist remark, and I don't blame her either. What a jerk.

"I am not afraid of that. Besides she could probably beat the two of us with all the crazy martial arts stuff that she does. I have seen how strong she is. I once saw her lift a fifty-pound bag of flour that she was buying for her grandmother. She carried it on her shoulder like it was nothing." Colomba's hurt expression quickly fades into a smile of gratitude. Alex, on the other hand, just seems amused by what I have said.

"Yeah, yeah, good excuse Louie. I didn't think you were such a wimp that you wouldn't even accept a fun challenge like this." I feel my heart pound in my anger at hearing him call me a wimp.

"Colomba, can I see the hammer please?" Colomba's smile disappears as she silently gives me the hammer. Is that disappointment in her eyes? I don't let myself think about that as I face the tower, lifting the hammer over my shoulder like how Colomba did it a minute ago. I suddenly feel sick. I take a deep breath before I swing down the hammer with all of my might. The metal bar flies up the tower and stops only halfway up. I didn't even make it close to where Colomba was. I stand there for a moment, not wanting to turn around and see Alex's gloating face. I hand the hammer back to the man running the game before I swallow my pride and look at Colomba and Alex. Alex has the gloating, proud face I expected, but Colomba's expression hurts me the most. She looks like she is pitying me. I never wanted to see that on her face, I don't want her to pity me. I am such a loser.

"Oh, too bad Louie. Might want to try working out a bit more." Colomba looks shocked by his words and she opens her mouth to say something, but Alex stops her before she can say what's on her mind by walking away from her and giving the man running the game the money to play. The man hands Alex the hammer, which he sets down for a moment. I am confused for a second before I realize that he is just trying to show off to Colomba. He rolls up his short-sleeved shirt so that his muscular arms can be seen better. I suddenly feel like hiding my own weak arms from view, but I don't want to look like an even bigger loser, so I just look away to seem like I'm not interested. Alex picks the hammer back up, swings the hammer over his head, and slams it down on the little button, sending the little piece of metal flying all the way to the top and ringing the bell. I lower my eyes, feeling ashamed. He did this on purpose. He knew that if he challenged me like that then I would accept his challenge and lose while he looks like the winner. Why was I stupid enough to fall for this? Why am I such an idiot?

"Good job man," the guy running the game says enthusiastically, "pick out any prize that you want." Alex doesn't waste a moment, he points to a large, stuffed purple poodle which the guy running the game gives him. Alex turns to Colomba with an overly pleasant smile. He holds out the fluffy stuffed animal to her.

"Here, a cute little prize for a cute little lady." Colomba accepts the dog with a smile, but my gloomy mood disappears a little when I see that her smile seems pretty uncomfortable.

"Thank you, Alex. That's very sweet of you." Alex smiles down at her warmly, not really seeing how she is obviously not comfortable with the gift.

She holds the poodle close to her, but she keeps her eyes down, as if she doesn't want to look at Alex. The three of us walk away from the tower and I'm glad, I never want to see that thing again. The three of us spend the last hour of the fair riding on a couple rides. I'm glad to say that whenever the ride only allowed two people to sit next to each other, Colomba always picked me instead of Alex to sit beside her.

Now that the night has ended, the three of us wait at the entrance to the fair for our rides home. As we talk, Alex glances over to a poster on the side of the ticket booth. I look over at it too to see that it is telling everybody about the dance that they have on the final night of the fair. My stomach feels like a block of ice. I completely forgot that they have this. I haven't gone to the fair since I was a kid because I didn't want to go alone since I didn't have any friends, but I can't believe that I let myself forget something like this. I have heard people talking about the end of the fair dance and, apparently, people think it is pretty important and fun. When Alex looks away from the poster down to Colomba, I already know what he wants to say before the words even leave his lips.

"Oh, look at that. The end of the fair dance will be here tomorrow night. I hope I can find someone to take with me. I don't want to look like a loser dancing by myself." I notice that Alex glances over at me for a second when he says loser, but I don't let that bother me since Colomba clearly shows her disinterest in what Alex is clearly implying. She looks up at him with a simple smile that masks some hidden anger.

"I'm sure you'll find someone to dance with. I'm sure you'll have a good time even if you dance by yourself." She leaves it at that without another word, leaving Alex to look surprised by her quick dismissal of him. Obviously, he expected her to be excited about the thought of him asking her to the dance. He tries to hide his disappointment, but I can see it in his eyes, and I love it.

My heart leaps a little in my chest as a thought pops into my head. If she doesn't want to go with him, would she want to go with me? I've never actually gone to a dance with a girl before. I would be the happiest guy on the face of the earth if she would be the first date to a dance I've ever had. I'm tempted to ask her now, but her father pulls up in his car to pick her up, ruining the moment. She steps into the car and leaves Alex and I alone in a tense, awkward silence. Alex glares at me when he sees the smile that I am trying to hold back.

"What are you so happy about?"

"Oh, nothing. Nothing at all. I guess I just had a good time at the fair." I am saved from the jaws of death by my uncle, who pulls up the car right in front of me. I practically leap into the front seat before Alex has a chance to do anything. On the ride home, I tell my Uncle Diego about everything that happened at the fair, except of course my failure with that tower game with Alex. I will never tell him about that.

I watch the trees fly past us as we drive down the road. The moon is almost full, casting an eerie light down on the town beneath it. It almost feels like I'm going to burst with excitement at the thought that I will be seeing Colomba tomorrow at the fair and I can ask her to the dance then. Different ways of asking her passes through my head as I try to come up with what to say. As I think through one possibility after another, the obvious problem pops into my head and overshadows all of the beautiful things I had been thinking about before. What if she says no? My heart, that had been only full of hope a moment ago, is now darkened and full of misery.

Why would she say yes? Who would say yes to go to a dance with a loser like me? I lower my gaze from the window as all hope leaves me.

# <u>Chapter Eleven</u>
## Colomba-
## Racing Thoughts

Even though it is getting pretty late, and I am getting changed into my pajamas to go to bed, I do not feel tired at all. Thoughts just keep swirling through my mind constantly, and I don't see any sign of them stopping. I just got home a little bit ago, but with all my racing thoughts it feels like hours have passed since I walked through the front door.

I can't believe everything that has happened tonight. Who could do something so cruel like that to Shay? I mean putting gum in someone's hair right before a beauty contest, that is just petty and terrible. Anybody could tell you how terrible getting gum in your hair is, so why would they do it to somebody else? Nobody even really knows Shay around here since she is always bouncing from one city to the next for her modeling, so why are they hurting her if they don't even know her? I only know her a little bit, but she seems like an incredibly sweet person, and a very smart girl.

What I said to her earlier is true though, I think everyone is just jealous of her. Girls as pretty as her always get the attention of the boys, people want to be near them, and good things tend to happen to good looking people. That's the way the world works, you would have to be blind not to see that. These girls see these facts too, and they are jealous of any girl that they think is prettier than them. It is a sad thing to see, and I can only hope and pray that these cruel pranks on Shay will just stop.

My mind is also going through what happened after Alex joined me and Luis. For a while now I have been thinking about Alex, but not in a good way. He has always been so nice to me, but several people in my life have been warning me about him. Luis, Nat, and even my grandma have started to tell me that Alex is bad news and I am really starting to believe them. I have always tried to keep good thoughts in my head about Alex since he has always been kind to me, and I haven't seen him do anything bad to anybody else, but that has changed tonight.

Anyone with eyes could see how he was being mean to Luis. When everyone was picking on me last year, when they thought that I was siding with the Crow, Luis avoided me for a little bit because he got involved in something that he didn't want me to get involved with. I'm not sure what it was, I never pushed him into giving me an explanation, but when he did start hanging out with me again Alex told me that Luis is the Crow. My grandma said that he was probably lying since it's obvious that Alex likes me a lot and he doesn't want other guys hanging out with me.

Apparently, he also wants to humiliate guys who hang out with me too judging from what he did with that one game at the fair. It was obvious that Luis didn't want to play, but Alex pushed him into it, basically calling him a coward and insulting me while doing it. He seemed so amused that Luis didn't want to play the game because he thought that Luis didn't want to get beaten in the game by a girl.

I know that I am stronger than most people would expect from my size. I am able to do a lot of things despite my size because of all the martial arts I have done over the years. Most people don't recognize this even after they have known me for a while. Luis is different though. He even stood up for me with Alex when he was teasing me. Luis is such a good guy. I am glad that he is my friend. It hurt me so much to see Alex humiliating him like that. I wanted to say something, I really did, but I couldn't think of the words at the time. I was just so frustrated by how Alex was treating me that I couldn't think straight. I just hope that Luis isn't mad at me for not sticking up for him.

I look over to the purple poodle stuffed animal that Alex gave me for winning the game. The little toy is sitting on top of my dresser, staring at me with its dark, dead eyes. I feel a bit uncomfortable just looking at it. I know what Alex was trying to tell me by giving me that doll as well as talking about the dance. He wants me to go to the end of the fair dance with him. After what he did with Luis, as well as all the warnings people have been giving me, I will never go out with him. He may act kind to me, but I now know what he is like underneath what he shows to me. I don't want him to be in any part of my life. I would never date him like he so clearly wants. From now on, whenever he comes near me, I will be polite, but I will not be friendly. I can only hope that he can take a hint and start to leave me alone.

I may not want to date while I am in school since I want to focus on classes and all that so I can get into a good college, but even if I was I wouldn't want to be with someone like Alex. He is always showing off about how athletic and rich he is and he never stops talking. He doesn't seem like a very intelligent guy, and not a very kind one either. Whenever I think about the guy I want to be with one day, I imagine a kind, intelligent, creative person who can be a good listener, but can speak when they want. I want someone who will treat me with respect and someone I can feel safe around. Someone like Luis, but Luis and I are just friends so I probably shouldn't think of him like that at all. I don't think he likes me in that way, so I just need to forget that. Too bad though. He really is such a good guy.

Before I settle myself in bed, I make sure to turn the purple poodle around so it isn't staring at me. I lie under the covers, eager for tomorrow since I know that I will be seeing my friends again at the fair in the evening. Hopefully this time though, I won't have to deal with Alex.

# Chapter Twelve
## Luis-
## More Trouble

It is the middle of the day right now, and I am finishing up folding my laundry in my room while talking to Shadow. Every once in a while, I impatiently look at the clock. I'm going to be meet Colomba and Nat at the fair in about two hours and the wait is killing me. I am so bored right now that I can't stand it. When I am done folding and putting away the last shirt in my pile, I lay down on my bed and turn on the little television that sits on top of my dresser. I always have my television set on the news, so it doesn't surprise me when I see the news channel come on. What does surprise me though is that there is a picture of me as the Crow in the corner of the screen beside the newscaster who is speaking. I sit up straight on my bed, my attention immediately taken.

"It has been months since the Crow has

made an attack on Drew's Hollow High School. It is unclear as to why he has disappeared, but that has not stopped the residents of the small town from worrying about him returning." The image on the screen changes to, what looks like an interview with the mayor (also known as the principal of my school). Just like always, he looks calm and collected while talking to the press.

"More than anything, we want the children of our town to be safe." Wow, spoken like a real politician. "We are preparing in every way we can for the new school year to start. We are making sure that when the Crow does come again, we will be ready for him. There is no need to worry about the safety of your children. We will be training all of the teachers and staff from the school in a new procedure for the unlikely possibility that the Crow does come back. With this procedure we can assure the safety of all the students in the school." The image of the mayor vanishes so that the newscaster can return to the screen. While the newscaster drones on and on about the new procedures that the principal was talking about, I look over to Shadow who is watching the news attentively.

"Do you think it's a bit weird that they think that they can protect themselves against something magical that they know absolutely nothing about?" Shadow shrugs her wings.

"I guess it is understandable. They are just trying to make themselves feel better about something they have no control over. They're just trying their best." I nod my head while I hide the smile that's threatening to appear on my face.

Sometimes Shadow sounds like a therapist or something when she talks. It's kind of funny. Maybe she could do that as a part-time job. I choke down a laugh at the thought of someone telling all their problems to a crow. My laughter completely dies and the smile disappears from my face when I realize that I am someone who tells all their problems to a crow.

My attention returns to the news when the picture of me as the Crow is replaced by a picture of Silver Dove.

"Even though the villain who calls himself the Crow has not been spotted for several months, that has not stopped our town's hero, Silver Dove, from protecting us. Just last week, Silver Dove was seen carrying several people out of a burning building and then helped the firemen put out the flames. She then left the scene before she was able to be interviewed for this station. Some other notable things that Silver Dove has done since the disappearance of the Crow are stopping several burglaries, helping some builders fix the city's bridge, and rescuing a small child who had fallen into an old well. Hopefully this hero can remain with us for as long as possible." I switch off the television, not wanting to listen to them praise Silver Dove any more.

"That's enough of that for right now, I guess." I say to Shadow, trying to make me turning off the television while they were talking about Silver Dove seem like nothing. As if having them praise her so much doesn't irritate me. Shadow seems to see through my little act, but she doesn't say anything about it. For that I'm grateful. Instead, she chooses to change the subject. I am not happy about the new subject she has chosen though.

"So, what are you going to do about the dance?" I close my eyes as I release a sigh.

"I don't know what you mean." Shadow rolls her dark eyes at me.

"Oh please, you know that you can't lie to me. Are you going to ask Colomba to the dance or not?" I try not to look at her as I give her the honest answer.

"She would never say yes to me. Why would a girl like her go out with a guy like me?"

"Because you treat her kindly." I turn around to face her, completely shocked by her words. "You listen to her and respect her. You are mature and can hold an intelligent conversation with her. Trust me, that is what any self-respecting girl wants. I should know, I am a girl too." I smile as hope begins to sink into me.

"You really think so?" Shadow chuckles at me.

"Of course. Being with someone isn't like what they show in the movies. It really isn't about the romance or being attractive. Being with someone is all about being able to talk to each other in a respectful way, being kind to one another, and wanting the best for each other. I believe that you and Colomba have that already, so why not take a chance and try?" Reaching over to her, I gently wrap my arms around Shadow to hold her close to me in a gentle embrace.

"Thank you, Shadow."

"You're very welcome. You have made me very proud of you today." I release her from my embrace so that I can look her in the face.

"You're proud of me because I'm going to ask Colomba to a dance?" She chuckles and shakes her head.

"Yes and no. I am proud that you are going to overlook your fear to ask her, but I am also proud of what you did the other day. You were able to fix the problem with the mayor and the judge trying to fix that competition. You did it without causing anybody harm or struggle. I think you handled it very well Master."

"Thank you, Shadow. I had a hard time figuring out how I was going to do it, but I think that I won't have any problems doing it this way. Nobody would dare to mess with the Crow and I doubt that the mayor will try to do anything else with any of the other judges since he knows that the Crow is watching him. I can only hope that whoever has been messing with Shay will stop. She really is a nice girl and I hate to see all this happen to her. Maybe it is time for the Crow to come back. Maybe those girls in the competition need to learn that they can't hurt an innocent person without being punished." I look to Shadow to see if she will give me an answer.

"If that is what you think is best, you know that I will follow you. I just need you to promise me that you will think through every part of your plan before you start it. Can you do that for me?" I take a moment, thinking over what she means by the promise she wants me to make.

"Shadow, I promise that I will think it through and try my best to make sure that everybody gets what they deserve."

# Chapter Thirteen
## Colomba-
## The Third
## Night

The world around me is alive with bright lights and chaotic noise, just like every night at the fair has been. Today is the last day of the fair though. It is kind of sad, but also pretty wonderful. At the end of the night they will announce all of the winners for the competitions and there is also the dance. This fair is always a wonderful way to end summer break. I love coming every year and I look forward to it for the next summer as soon as it is over.

I can only hope that Luis and I will win a few ribbons. The two of us have worked so hard, and I think that Luis really deserves to win something. He is such an amazing artist. He needs to be recognized for his talent. He doesn't seem to have a lot of confidence in most things. Hopefully, if he can win something then he might realize that he does have talent and gain some confidence from that. I want him to be happier.

I meet up with Luis and Nat so that we can all enjoy the last day of the fair together. We enjoy around an hour of fun together before something happens that brings a dark cloud over all three of us. Nat notices it first and her smile disappears. When Luis and I see her sudden change in mood, we turn around to find out why she didn't look happy anymore and we quickly got our answer. Alex is walking toward the three of us now with a confident smile on his face. My heart feels like it is my throat and it is pounding. Oh gosh, what's going to happen now?

"Hey guys, you interested in having an extra person in your group?" Alex says this as if he expects us to say yes, like we want him to have fun with us. Does he not remember what he did last night? Why would we want to hang out with him after he so clearly tried to humiliate Luis? What is wrong with this guy? Luis seems to share my opinion since he glares at Alex, but I am the one to answer Alex's question.

"No thanks Alex. We were just about to do something together if you don't mind." I don't wait for a reply. I just walk away, taking Luis and Nat's hands and leading them away from him. Trying to get away from him as fast as I can through the crowded fair.

"Wow Birdy, I've never seen you do something like that before." I stop so that I can look at Nat and talk. We are far enough from Alex now that I feel safe to speak freely.

"Well after the way he spoke to Luis last night, he doesn't deserve to hang out with us." Nat smiles at me and holds up her hand for a high five.

"Nice, glad you finally see him the way the rest of us do." I chuckle as I give her the high five.

"Thanks, I really appreciate that. Now let's go have some fun." The next two hours are spent doing all the crazy stuff people do at fairs; we ride a bunch of rides that make us feel like throwing up, we eat junk food even though our stomachs still feel a bit queasy, and we joke and laugh with each other until we have a hard time breathing. It was amazing. Of course, it didn't last. What a surprise.

As the three of us were heading into the competition tent to see how Shay is doing before the final part of her competition, I heard someone call my name. I turn around to see Alex running up to me. A sigh leaves me as I turn toward Nat and Luis.

"You guys head in. I'll see what he wants." They both leave me pretty reluctantly, but I wait until they are both out of my sight before I speak to Alex.

"What's up Alex?" He looks surprised, as if he can't believe I'm asking this.

"'What's up', you're really asking me that? What happened earlier? Why did you blow me off like that?" I glare at him and he takes a step back in shock. I have never shown him anything but kindness before, must be kind of scary to see me angry with him. Usually, I would feel bad for making him uncomfortable, but right now I don't care.

"I blew you off because I didn't want to be near you. You were mean to Luis last night and I don't want to be around anyone who insults my friends. Goodbye." I turn around to follow Luis and Nat into the tent, but Alex stops me with one question.

"Why are you friends with him anyway?" I immediately stop walking to look at him, now it is my turn to be shocked.

"What did you just say?" He walks closer to me, knowing that he has my complete attention.

"Why are you friends with that freak?" I am stunned into silence, and he takes advantage of it by continuing to talk. "I mean he is an absolute loser, why do you waste your time with him? He's boring, he's a wimp, and he's so awkward. Nobody even likes him." I walk up so close to him that we are almost nose to nose. I glare at him with all of the anger I have inside of me. His frightened expression has returned to his face.

"I like him Alex, I care about Luis. He is one of my best friends. He is not boring; he is actually a very funny guy and he is fun to be around. He is not a wimp, just because he isn't as athletic as you doesn't mean that he's weak. And he isn't awkward, he's a very shy guy but once you get to know him he is such a lovable person. I'm sorry that you aren't able to see that and can only judge him on the surface. Hopefully you can one day see past your own egotistical nose and learn how to see people as they truly are and not in the close-minded way you view them now." I turn away from him and head inside, not even looking back when he calls my name. I just keep walking.

A little bit of guilt comes over me as I keep walking. I should have said all of that in a nicer way. I know that he has not been a very nice person recently, and probably always hasn't been a very nice person, but that doesn't mean that I should be mean right back to him. I should be the bigger person and not stoop to his level. Should I apologize? I don't know about that. Would that seem like giving in to him and he would try to get close to me again? Arrg this is awful. Why is dealing with people so hard? People are so confusing!

I try to keep Alex out of my mind as I meet up with Nat and Luis who are waiting for me inside. As soon as he saw me come in, Luis asked if I was alright. He really is such a sweet guy. I tell him that I am alright, that Alex just wanted an explanation for earlier and I told him that I didn't want to be around anyone who insults my friends. Luis beams at me in his happiness at hearing me refer to him as my friend.

The three of us head to the area of the tent where all the girls are preparing for the contest, which will start in a little less than an hour. All around us, girls are busily doing their hair and looking over their dresses and other costumes within various mirrors for the talent portion of the competition tonight. From across the tent I can see Shay giving herself one last look over in the mirror before she notices the three of us. She gives us a big smile as she comes over to greet us. She is wearing a beautiful white dress that trails behind her. She looks as glamorous as a movie star in that dress.

I'm about to smile back at her when the unnerving feeling that something bad is about to happen sends a brick of ice into my stomach. When I was first given my pin, my grandmother told me that I would develop a sense to detect if something bad is about to happen. That sense is now going haywire. I glance around the room to try to find any kind of threat, but I only see the other girls in the contest. As I look at them though I start to notice that something is kind of strange with how they are acting. Several of them are carrying cans of soda, I can actually see a few of them shaking the cans. Why on earth are they doing that? Everybody knows that you shouldn't shake a soda can. I also notice something else weird. All of the ones who are holding a soda can are all heading in the same direction. They are all walking toward Shay with a determined look in their eyes. What they are planning quickly comes into my head and I try to shout out a warning, but I am not fast enough.

All of the girls holding soda cans suddenly rush toward Shay and open the cans, pointing the spray of soda directly at Shay. Shay gives out a terrified shriek as she tries to cover her face from the sugary shower she is receiving. As soon as the soda has run out of the cans, the girls surrounding Shay throw the empty cans at her before running off to be lost in the crowd of other girls before anybody in charge could see who they are and catch them. All of this only took a few seconds, but the damage is still very bad.

Shay lowers her hands from her face to look at the damage. Her beautiful dress is now stained in a rainbow of colors from the soda. Her hair hangs in wet tangles around her head, and her makeup is running down her face. The soda dripping down her face is now joined by her tears. After everything these girls have done to her, this is something that I can't help her fix. There isn't any time to clean her up and get the stains from her dress, and she can't go up on stage like that.

Shay stands where she is for a moment while the entire tent has fallen silent as they stare at her with either looks of complete shock or happiness. Some of the girls are happy watching this completely innocent girl getting hurt. They are happy that the girl they are jealous of feels miserable. Shay's body shakes a little as she begins to sob. She runs out of the tent as fast as she can while I chase after her. I run as fast as my feet can carry me, but she has a head start on me. I rush out of the tent and look around myself to try and find her. Countless people pass by me as they go to either a ride, a game, or a food stand. I see a few people I recognize and many that I don't, but I can't find the one I am looking for. I can't find Shay within the crowd. I have lost her the moment when I feel as if she needed me the most.

# <u>Chapter Fourteen</u>
## Luis-
## Justice for
## Shay

Nat and I watch as Colomba runs out of the tent after Shay. Almost all of the girls in the tent laugh as the two of them leave, completely amused by their cruel prank. One of them tells everyone that she took a video of all that on her phone and she's going to post it on A-Streamer. What is wrong with these people? I can tell from Nat's face that she wants to say something to all of them but is afraid to say it. Nat may be confident around Colomba and I, but she is terrified of speaking to people she doesn't know. I am terrified of speaking up for Shay in front of all these people too, but that doesn't mean that I can't help her.

"Hey Nat, I don't think that Colomba is going to find her. How about you get Colomba and the two of you wait here in case Shay comes back and I will go around the fair to try and find her." Nat thinks about it for a moment before she goes out to bring Colomba back in while I go out a different exit. I will find Shay, but not to help her in the way that Nat or Colomba probably expects.

I think that the Crow has been dormant long enough. It is time for him to make a comeback. I left so that people would begin to remember how things were like before I came, people always hurting each other without a thought. All those girls who have hurt Shay, as well as the mayor and the judge he tried to bribe, they are all against her just because she is pretty. They have all forgotten what I am here for. They have forgotten what I am capable of doing. They will soon be reminded of my power.

As soon as I have found a quiet spot hidden behind some boxes around the back of the competition tent, I place my hand over the Crow Medal and Shadow appears to me, perched on top of one of the boxes.

"Hello Master. How can I help you?" I smile at her, feeling excited like I always do whenever I am about to become the Crow to help the other kids like me.

"Transform me Shadow. It's time for Shay to get what she deserves." Shadow doesn't say anything, she merely starts flying around me in a circle. I close my eyes, enjoying the thought that I am finally coming back. I will finally be myself again, my true self. I open my eyes only a moment later to find myself as the Crow. I feel my hands tightening into fists at my side within the black gloves of my costume. It feels wonderful being this part of myself again. It has been too long. Closing my eyes, I whisper, "Shadow, find Shay."

I watch through Shadow's eyes as she flies through the fair. More people than I could count pass by Shadow without seeing her, but of course they don't, she is only a shadow. They are too busy trying to have fun to notice something so simple, yet so out of place as the shadow of a crow that isn't actually there. She flies through the fair, her shadow cast on tents and rides, until she flies into the competition tent.

As Shadow flies through the tent, I listen to the girls happily laughing and joking with each other about what they just did to Shay. I chuckle to myself as I think that they won't be laughing for much longer. Shadow carefully picks up the tiara that will be placed on the head of the winner of the beauty contest. I have plans for this little piece of plastic. Shadow flies past Colomba and Nat who are sitting on some chairs, waiting and hoping that Shay will come back. Shadow knows where she is though. She flies straight through the tent and to the other of the tent, down a hill into a grassy field, to find Shay sitting on a large rock. Her eyes are now red from her tears while she reeks of sugary sodas. Shadow flies into her heart, taking the little crown inside with her, and I announce my presence to her.

Hello Shay. She immediately stops crying as she practically leaps to her feet and looks around herself, trying to find the voice that frightened her.

You don't need to be afraid. I will not hurt you. I am the Crow. I want to help you.

In her mind, she remembers someone telling her about how the Crow has been attacking the school, trying to defend the underdogs. A small bit of hope is beginning to replace her fear.

"How do you think you can help me?" I chuckle softly, making her quiver in terror.

I have seen how the other girls have been treating you in this competition. Their jealousy of you is turning them into beasts. I can help you show the world the beasts they truly are. I can give you the power to make them as ugly as they have acted, as ugly as their souls.

She perks up at the idea as she thinks of how those girls have been treating her. She wonders what I mean though when I say that I can make them as ugly as their souls, but she doesn't stop to think about it. She wants to get back at them, and she wants to get back at them now.

"Alright. Do whatever you have to do to help me get back at them. I will do whatever you say and be whoever you want me to be." I smile to myself in my joy. It is finally happening again. I missed this moment where I give these people what they truly want, revenge.

If you mean that and follow what I say, I will give you everything you want. Now let's get started.

The little plastic crown that Shadow had been carrying while she flew into Shay's heart is now sitting on top of Shay's soda-soaked hair. Shay's lips pull up into a smile. This smile isn't the pleasant, innocent smile that she had used on stage while in the competition. This one is full of hatred and joy knowing that she will get back at those girls who hurt her for a stupid plastic crown. Rays of light seem to be coming from her as Shadow begins to take her over. Even though the sun is just beginning to set on the horizon, it looks as if a new sun is forming in that little field. Shay is now as bright as a star in the sky.

# <u>Chapter Fifteen</u>
## Colomba-
## The Beauty
## Queen

Nat and I sit on some chairs, waiting and hoping that Shay will come back. Luis was kind enough to have Nat bring me back in while he searched for her. He is such a sweet guy. The other girls are laughing and joking about what just happened with Shay. What is wrong with these people? How can they joke about something so terrible? They must be completely heartless.

It is pretty calm within the tent as they all chat, but the calm is shattered in an instant. What feels like the strongest surge of wind I've ever felt rushes through the room through the only entrance to this part of the tent. It is so strong that my hair quickly rushes behind me and papers scatter around the room in a frenzy. The wind dies down very quickly to reveal something standing within the entryway of the tent. I can't quite see the figure clearly since they must be wearing something reflective since the dying sunlight is making them glow so brightly that I have to squint my eyes. Something about them must have scared Nat since she quickly gets out of her chair and tries to run away, taking me by the hand in the process. She drags me along for a few steps before I trip over a makeup bag that one of the girls in the contest was using. I fall to the ground while Nat runs around the mysterious figure and out the door.

The figure steps into the room and out of the sun so that they stop glowing and we can all clearly see them. I take in a gasp when I see what is standing before me, but not a gasp of fear or shock, but one in complete awe. What is standing above me is the most beautiful thing I have ever seen. A woman who appears to be made of solid gold stands beside me. She is wearing what looks like a Roman toga with a golden sash around her waist. Her hair that gently blows in the breeze appears to be made out of golden threads while her blue eyes are made of jewels. She almost looks like a golden statue of an ancient goddess, far more beautiful than any human could ever be. On top of her mass of golden curls sits what looks like a tiara fit for a princess. Something is familiar about that tiara though. My eyes grow wide when I realize where I have seen it before. It is the one being used for the beauty contest. When I take a closer look at the golden face there is no doubt who this girl is, Shay.

The golden girl stands in front of me and all of the contestants for the beauty contest, looking at all of them with a stony expression. Her jewel eyes scan the terrified crowd in front of her as if she is evaluating her prey.

"You all believe that you are beautiful," Her voice is soft, yet it carries around the tent and seems to echo in the strangest way. It is a voice that sounds almost unearthly, as if she is no longer human. "You believe that, and some others may believe it too, but I will show the world what you are like on the inside." Without warning, one of her golden hands shoots out and grabs one of the girls who had been standing close to her. The girl lets out a terrible scream that freezes the blood in my veins. The entire tent is filled with a golden light that is so bright I have to close my eyes. When I open them, I am shocked into silence at what I see.

Standing right where the girl was only a moment ago is a creature that is more hideous than anything I have ever seen. The figure is small, probably a little less than four feet tall and so terribly skinny that it almost looks like a half-starved animal. It is hunched over as if nobody ever taught it to stand up straight and now it permanently has bad posture. Its skin is shriveled and wrinkled like an old prune. The dry scaly skin is a sickening green color that makes my stomach churn. Yellowing teeth protrude from the lower lip that almost look like the tusks of a warthog. Its nose is long and hooked, similar to that of a cartoon witch. Warts are dotted all over its face. Coming from its mouth is a disturbing wheezing that makes me want to cover my ears.

What truly horrifies me though is that the

creature is wearing a dress, a familiar dress. The creature is wearing the exact same dress that the girl that the golden girl had touched only moments before had on. When I make that realization, it is easy to figure out what happened. The golden girl transformed that girl. She did as she promised. She made that girl as ugly as she had been acting. The creature looks at the people surrounding her, all of us staring at her in horror. The creature seems confused by this, but when it slowly lifts up its gnarly hands up to its face it understands. The poor creature releases a pitiful, mournful wail of despair that breaks the stillness in the air.

The silence doesn't last long after that creature's shriek. The other girls stare at the creature that had been an ordinary girl like themselves before they all start screaming all at once. They all try to run away from the golden girl, trying to escape through the only exit in the tent. The exit that is being blocked by the golden girl.

As they try to get past her, she merely has to touch them for them to transform just like the other girl. The tent is filled with screaming and crying as the girls look at their newly transformed selves in the mirror, horrified by what they see. It doesn't take long for every single one of the girls in the tent to be transformed into a hideous creature. I am the only one left. I know this and so does the golden girl. The mysterious golden figure stands above me, staring down at me with those blue jewel eyes.

"You have a beautiful soul. You were not cruel like these other girls. For that you will remain as you are. You will not be punished. Spread the word about what has happened here. Let the world know that the Beauty Queen will show everyone whether or not their souls are as beautiful as they believe."

With that said she starts to walk out of the tent, but one of her newly transformed creatures stops her by grabbing onto her flowing robe.

"You can't keep us like this forever!" The little creature's voice is gravely and deep. "Change us back!" The Beauty Queen just smirks down at the creature in front of her.

"You got what you deserved, but if you follow me and do as I say then I might transform you back." She snatches her robe out of the creature's grasp and walks out. All of the creatures follow after her, eager to be turned back into their normal selves. They all leave while I am left alone, staring after them with open mouthed shock. Did that actually just happen in front of me? The Crow has always given his people powers, but he has never had a person who could transform others. This is just plain freaky. There is no doubt in my mind though that the person I just saw was Shay. I guess that is time again for Silver Dove to make an appearance to kick the Crow's butt yet again.

Since nobody else is here, I place my hand over the Dove Pin and say the magic words, "Peaceful warrior." I transform almost instantly, and I don't waste any time. I open my wings and fly out the door and soar over the crowd of people at the fair who are now running around in chaos while the strange creatures the Beauty Queen created are attacking people and wrecking the place. I can see one creature clinging to a woman's back while pulling at her hair. A man tries to beat the creature off the woman's back with a piece of broken wood, but the creature remains firmly in place while the woman screams in terror and pain. Apparently the first order she has given her little minions is to attack innocent people. I can only imagine what she will have them do to me as soon as she sees me.

It doesn't take me long to find the Beauty Queen from my view from the sky. You know, it is pretty easy to find a solid gold person out of a group of regular people. She is walking through the fair, grabbing at anybody she can reach so that they turn into monsters too in a split second so that she can grab someone else. I fly toward her as fast as I can. I don't even slow down as I fly into her, sending her soaring through the air and into a pile of crates. They all shatter into planks and splinters while the Beauty Queen slowly picks herself up, a scowl on her beautiful golden face.

"Attack Silver Dove my monsters!" All of her little creatures suddenly stop what they're doing and run toward me, eager to please the girl who has power over them. They leap all over me, their tiny, bony hands trying to rip off the feathers of my wings. What they don't know is that I am invincible. They can't hurt me. I flick a few of them off my wings as easily as if they were bugs. I try to gently move them off me, not wanting to hurt them since I know that they are just desperate people who want to return to their normal selves. They do not show me any mercy though. In my desperation, I start ripping them off of me and throwing them a small distance away, still trying not to hurt them. They release their feral, wheezing growls in my ears as they try to rip off my helmet so that they can attack my face, but I don't let them even get close to it. I throw them off of me as soon as they try. Once I have gotten one of them off of me, another one takes its place.

I have just ripped off the billionth little creature from my head, and another one of them has decided to take advantage of the opportunity of having a clear shot at my head. I notice it too late, but one of the creatures picks up a piece of broken wood that looks as if it had been part of a crate and swings it at my head like a baseball bat. The piece of wood snaps against my helmet, sending a shower of wooden shards all over the ground. My helmet makes a horrible ringing sound from the impact and it echoes through my skull. I am tempted to rip off the helmet just to get rid of that nauseating sound, but that would be stupid. Okay, now I'm really mad.

I need to figure out a way to get these guys out of the picture so that I can focus on the Beauty Queen. As soon as they are all off me for the moment, I fly high in the air to make sure that they can't get to me. I look around at the fair below me, trying to figure out a solution to the problem. Below me, people are hiding in tents or trying to make it to their cars so that they can escape while all the little creatures are growling and hissing up at me. They all want me to come down so that they can try and take me down again. Looking over at a fallen tent, an idea suddenly enters my mind and a smile appears behind my mask.

I quickly fly toward the fallen tent and examine one corner to find a long rope attached to it. Taking the rope in my hand, I rush over to the other three corners of the tent and tie the rope to them. Running over to the middle of the flattened tent on the ground, I hold the middle of the rope in a tight grip. I take in a deep breath before I yell out for everyone to hear, "Come and get me! I'm right here waiting for you!"

It only takes a moment for a mass of the little creatures to come out from behind a tent and run toward me, their pointed little teeth flashing in the dying sunlight. Even though every fiber of my being is telling me to run from these frightening creatures, I stand my ground and wait for them. I wait until all of them are almost so close they can touch me, until they are all standing on top of the fallen tent. As soon as the final one has stepped onto the tent, I shoot straight into the air, still holding onto the rope. With the rope still attached to the corners of the tent, I lift the tent up in the air with me, carrying all of the little creatures in the tent and unable to get out. Okay now that I have them, I need a place to put them where they won't get in my way. From the corner of my eye, I spot the Ferris Wheel and a smile comes onto my face. I fly over to it and tie the rope to the little seat on the top of the Ferris Wheel, suspending all the creatures in the tent almost thirty feet in the air. From inside the tent I can hear them screaming at me to let them out.

"Trust me guys, you would rather stay in there. The fall is a bit of a doozy. Just wait patiently until I have all this sorted out." I fly away to head back to the Beauty Queen to end this as quickly as possible, before she messes with anybody else. When I have her in my sights, I dive right at her, feet first. She turns around just in time to see me as I fly right into her stomach with my feet. She crashes to the ground while I leap off of her.

"Turn all those girls back and give up these powers that the Crow has given you. Shay you should know that this is not what you should do." Unlike everyone else I have confronted with powers from the Crow, she doesn't bother to ask me how I know her real name. She just glares at me from her position on the ground.

"Why should I?! They got what they deserved and so will you! You have foiled the Crow's plans long enough! I will take care of you now!" I know that I should probably be more intimidated by her threat, but all I can do is chuckle as I respond to her.

"Foiled? Who says foiled anymore?" The Beauty Queen's hands turn into fists as she picks herself up from the dirt.

"I will make everyone see you as you truly are! I will make everyone see just how ugly your soul is, just like the rest of them!" My heart stops as she starts running toward me. She's going to turn me into one of those little creatures too. I quickly dodge her hand that she was aiming at my shoulder. I drop to the ground and swing my leg out toward her legs, sweeping them out from under her. She falls to the ground and I leap out of the way as she tries to swing her hand out toward me as she falls.

How on earth am I going to beat her if I can't even get close to her since she might touch me? I need to find a way to tie her up or something, like what I did with the creatures.

I look around to try and find something to subdue her with, but there is nothing around me but scraps of trash and debris from when her little creatures were wrecking the place. She picks herself up again and the two of us start doing, what probably looks like, a very weird dance. She tries to move in and touch me so that she can transform me while I move out of the way, only an inch or so from her fingers.

I duck down to avoid one of her strikes to see a long metal tube. I have no idea what it is used for, but I know how I am going to use it. I grab it as fast as I can and swing it at her shoulder. The impact creates a ringing sound of metal on metal. This doesn't really seem to cause her any pain, but she definitely looks annoyed. I glance down at the metal tube to see that it is now bent very badly. It is useless to me.

*"You've got to be kidding me!"* I toss the bent tube down so that the Beauty Queen and I can continue our strange dance of her reaching out to grab me, and me trying desperately to get out of her way while trying to figure out another way of striking back at her without getting too close. I am tempted to take out my sword to strike at her with, but I don't know if she's invincible like me. I don't want to risk killing her. I can't keep this up forever, sooner or later she is going to be able to get ahold of me. She proves that theory almost immediately after

it pops into my mind.

One hand shoots forward toward my stomach, which I easily dodge, but I didn't see her other hand come forward straight toward my face. Before I even noticed it, the hand wrapped around the only portion of my face that isn't covered by my mask. A sudden light that seems to be coming from me forces me to close my eyes.

No, no, no, no! This wasn't supposed to happen! Now that I am going to become one of these creatures. I probably won't have my powers as Silver Dove and I won't be able to defeat her, the Crow will win. I have failed. After all my training and all the time dedicated to becoming Silver Dove, I have failed. After a moment, I open my eyes, getting ready to accept my fate when I see something that surprises me. The Beauty Queen has stepped back in surprise, her jewel eyes open wide in shock. I glance down at my hands to see if I have changed into something unusual, but I am confused by what I see.

Turning my head to the side, I look at myself in the mirror in one of the tents selling jewelry. I now understand why the Beauty Queen is so surprised. Standing in my place appears to be a statue of Silver Dove made out of actual silver. Bright blue gemstones shine where my eyes are, and I sparkle even in the dim light of the almost faded sun. I look toward the Beauty Queen and I understand. Her power is to show on the outside what people are like on the inside. All of those girls from the contest acted like ugly monsters, and that's what they became. I, on the other hand, did not. I did everything I could to help her when she was struggling, just like I do for everyone I see. Now everyone can see my soul, but mine is beautiful.

I can hear the Beauty Queen's golden hands creating a horrible metallic scraping sound as her fingers curl into fists. Now that she can see that her powers won't work on me, she swings her fist forward to try and hit my face. I block it easily and our two metal arms clang together as I do so. She keeps sending one punch after another that I block. The entire area is filled with the sounds of our metal arms banging against each other. It almost sounds as if a person is ringing a gong over and over again. As her fury grows, her fists keep swinging faster and faster, but with my years of training I barely have to try and block her strikes.

As my irritation spreads, I decide to stop defending and attack instead. While one hand blocks her strike, my other fist flies forward and hits her squarely in the face, creating a satisfying clanging sound. She topples to the ground in a heap while I stand over her. I look down at the Beauty Queen, feeling completely confident now.

"Since we both can clearly see that you have no power over me, are we going to keep doing this weird, pointless battle or are we going to talk?" She tries to get up fast, and I can tell that she is going to try and run away. I prevent that easily. I unsheathe my sword and impale it through her toga and into the ground, pinning her to the spot. "Okay yeah, we're going to talk."

"I don't want to talk to you." She growls furiously while I look down at her with annoyance.

"I know, I could tell by the way you kept trying to punch me in the face." I sigh, trying to get rid of my annoyance so that I can try and talk her down. To make her see that I'm not the bad guy.

"Shay, I know that you have been going through a lot just because those girls in the contest are jealous of you. You can't let that get the better of you so that you try and hurt others." She kicks at my sword in the ground, trying to loosen it, but it barely even moves from her strike.

"Why not?! They deserved it didn't they?! They acted ugly, so why not let the world see them that way! They all think that I have a perfect life because everyone thinks that I am pretty, they all hate me because of that and-"

"Yeah and whoever says that it is easier living life as a pretty person is an idiot!" I interrupt, not wanting her rant to go on forever and ruin everybody's final evening at the fair. "Nobody's life is easy no matter what they look like! Just because a person is pretty doesn't mean that they don't have problems too. It also doesn't mean that people can hurt you just because you are prettier than them. It doesn't give them the excuse. It also doesn't give you the excuse to hurt them just because they hurt you. Just because somebody acts ugly to you doesn't mean you have to be ugly right back." The golden girl stares up at me with surprise at how harshly I am speaking.

"Let me tell you something very important." I kneel down so that we are only a few feet away from each other, the two of us staring deeply into the other's eyes. "Your appearance is an accident."

She blinks rapidly in her confusion. "Yeah, good looks or bad looks are just an accident of nature. You weren't meant to be pretty while someone else wasn't, it is just what happened. No plan, no nothing, just an accident of genetics. Your appearance does not matter. Your appearance is just part of a body that was meant to live its life depending on what you are as a person, not a face, wants. No matter what you look like, you are the one making the decisions. You decide your own fate." I smile at her, finally letting a softer side of me show. Hoping that I can show her that I am not trying to be mean to her, I am just speaking honestly so that she can see the truth.

"Hopefully, one day, the rest of the world can realize this too and appearances won't really mean anything. The problem is that I don't think either of us will see that happen in our lifetimes. What matters for us now though is whether or not you will let their judgement of you, based on your appearance, affect you. Will you let them win, or will you just live your life the best you can and do what you want despite how you look and how people judge you?" She falls silent as she thinks about what I just said. After a moment of silence, she looks back up at me with curiosity.

"You sound as if you have experience with this; are you judged on how you look too?" I think back on all the comments people have made to me, especially Alex, about how small I am and how they doubt me with my martial arts training. How they all think that I am weak just because I don't look like the stereotypical tough girl. I smile at her.

"Isn't everyone?" The Beauty Queen finally smiles at me, realizing that we both share the same pain.

"I understand. I am done. I am ready for this to be over." She transforms instantly back into her usual self. She is no longer wet from the sodas that were sprayed on her, but her dress is still stained and her hair is a sticky mess. Well, I can fix that pretty easily. I place my hand over the dove emblem on my armor and say the magic words, "Bring peace little dove."

The dove on my armor flies off of my chest and straight up in the air. It goes up as high as the Ferris Wheel, and I use one of my wings to cover both me and Shay so that the blinding light does not hurt our eyes. When it is safe, I remove my wing from the both of us to reveal that the fair is back to the way it was only an hour ago, all the damage caused by the Beauty Queen's little creatures is gone. I smile when I look over at Shay to see that her dress is no longer stained, and she looks just as wonderful as she did before she was sprayed by the soda. I rest my hand on her shoulder as she glances down at herself, amazed by the transformation.

"You should head back to the competition tent. They will probably try to start the last part of the competition soon. I wish you luck." She simply nods and smiles at me before she runs off to the tent, eager to try and win. I fly off before anybody else can get the courage to come out of their hiding places to try and thank me. I don't want to be thanked for something that needs to be done. I fly to a nearby clump of trees so that I can have the privacy to transform back into my normal self and walk back to the fair to watch the final part of the competition.

# Chapter Sixteen
## Luis-
## The Judging

Colomba, Nat, and I walk out of the beauty competition with smiles on our faces. It was a surprise to nobody that Shay won the contest hands down.

I had to chuckle a bit when Angela heard that she lost and looked as if she was about to throw a hissy fit on stage. I was really hoping that would happen, but she managed to hold on to her poise for a few minutes before the contest officially ended and she marched off the stage with her nose in the air. She even pushed one girl out of the way as she was making her way to the stairs leading off the stage. I am always surprised by how much of a petty drama queen she is. It would be truly hilarious if I wasn't one of the people she targets whenever she's in a bad mood. Thankfully, the three of us got away before she even got near us and now we are heading to the other part of the competition tent where they have all the stuff that Colomba and I made. By now, everything has been judged.

As we walk over there, I think about what just happened only half an hour ago. So Silver Dove has defeated another one of my soldiers? I guess that since this has happened so many times before that I don't really feel that bad about it anymore. Either that or I'm just still pretty happy about everything that has been going on recently; Colomba modeling for my portrait, getting to hang out with Nat and Colomba during the fair, and, my favorite, having Colomba ditch Alex like she did. That part was really awesome. I think I will always cherish that memory. To be honest, even though Nat and I had been waiting inside the tent for her to talk to Alex, we listened in to make sure that she was alright. Nat knows how I feel about Colomba, and we both hate Alex, so we had a blast listening to her ditch him. We even silently high fived each other as it was happening. It was a beautiful moment.

I guess that I can't even consider what happened to Shay as a loss though. I mean, thanks to Silver Dove's power to fix stuff, Shay looked like she did before those girls sprayed her with soda and she was able to win the contest. So, I guess the past couple of days have been a win for everybody. Even if I don't win any ribbons at the contests, I will still feel happy because of everything that has happened. The three of us enter the tent to see many people looking over the items they had created, seeing whether or not they won anything. Some are disappointed while others are joyful at their accomplishment. My stomach suddenly turns to ice at the thought that I may be one of those disappointed people in a few moments. I will still be happy with everything that has happened, but I won't be as happy I suppose.

We decide to go check out Colomba and her grandmother's stuff first, just to be polite as well as since I am a bit nervous about seeing mine. It doesn't surprise any of us that Colomba and her grandmother got a ribbon on practically everything they made. All together, they got five ribbons. Four first place ribbons and one for third place. She called her grandmother to tell her the good news, and her grandmother told her that they could grab everything up once she comes over to pick her up at the end of the night. Now it is my turn.

The three of us walk over to the art tables for the contests. My palms feel like they are covered in a cold sweat and my heart is pounding. I'm going to lose, aren't I? Why did I even try to do this? When we make it to the art section I see someone that makes me stop thinking about me being a complete failure.

"Mr. Sizemore?" He turns around and smiles at me. Mr. Sizemore was always my favorite teacher. He teaches art and has always been kind to me. During class he would always compliment my drawings and is one of the only adults in my life who has ever treated me kindly and given me encouragement.

"Hello Luis. I was hoping that I would see you here. Have you found your art work yet?" I shake my head at him. "Well come on over. Yours are right over here. I was very happy to be chosen as one of the judges for the contest, I was even happier when I saw your work. We aren't allowed to know the names of the artists for fairness purposes, but when it was all over I was proud to see your name on a few items." My eyes grow wide.

"You're one of the judges?"

"Yep, but only for the art competitions. It was a lot of fun. Here is your stuff." He points to a small table to reveal all three of my drawings, each with a ribbon on it. My drawing of the crow has a ribbon for second place in the animal drawings competition, the tree drawing has a third place ribbon for landscape, and hanging from the corner of the frame for Colomba's portrait is a first place ribbon. My heart stops in my chest. I won? I actually won one of the most popular contests in this entire thing? I don't believe it. Colomba, on the other hand, is not surprised.

"Congratulations Luis! I knew you could do it!" She wraps her arms around me in a quick, tight hug while the disbelief finally begins to fade and happiness takes over.

"Oh my gosh, I didn't think I would win that one!" Oh my gosh, I am so happy that I feel like I could cry at any moment. I can't believe that I've actually won something. I don't think I've ever won anything in my life before this.

"You did a very impressive drawing of your girlfriend Luis. I can see a bright future in the art world for you." I notice Colomba blush beside me from when Mr. Sizemore called her my girlfriend.

"Thank you, Sir. Colomba is just a friend though. She was kind enough to model for the portrait." Mr. Sizemore smiles at the two of us knowingly.

"Oh my apologizes. I didn't mean to embarrass you two like that." Colomba smiles sweetly at him.

"It's alright, we understand. I'll be back in a little bit, I'm just going to collect the prize money for the stuff we made." As she leaves, the two of us remain silent for a moment before Mr. Sizemore says something that makes my heart leap.

"Luis, over my many years of being an artist, I have learned how to recognize many things in the work of other artists. When someone paints or draws a person they love there is a certain magic about their work. That is one of the reasons I voted for yours to be the winner. I can understand why you love her; she seems to be a very kind, gentle girl with life shining in her eyes. You may be friends now, but I wish you luck in making her your girlfriend." I smile at him, not even bothering to hide how I feel. I know that Mr. Sizemore can see right through me and isn't judging me on it. When he says that he is wishing me luck in this, he means it.

Without another word, I take all three of my ribbons off of my works and hold them in my hand, staring at them with pure joy. As I hold the ribbons in my hand, I think about the one ribbon that I didn't win because I didn't enter it in the competition. I had thought about joining the competition for song writing but I decided against it.

I did end up writing a song, but I didn't want to share it with anyone. What I ended up writing was far too personal, and I would be terrified of sharing that with anyone. The paper I wrote it down on is in my pocket, but I don't have to read it, I already have it memorized.

<u>Hero</u>

Some heroes wear capes
With lots of adoring fans
But baby all I want
Is just to hold your hand
I'd take a face punch or work to much
As long as you're with me

Some of us can fly
Others lift heavy things
But the greatest power in life
Is the love between you and me

Now I'm not a villain girl
But I will steal your heart
I'll hide it away
To bring a brand new start
I'll take a gut punch, or a kick to the knee
As long as you are here with me

Some of us can fly
Others lift heavy things
But the greatest power in life
Is the love between you and me

I'll do what it takes
To have you by my side
I'll jump every mountain
And turn every tide
You can hit me with a train, or drown me in the sea
I can take it all as long as you're with me

# <u>Chapter Seventeen</u>
## Colomba-
## One Last
## Dance

Nearly all of the people attending the fair are now gathered underneath a large pavilion. A large ring of people are on the outside, chatting and watching the people in the much clearer center of the pavilion where many couples are dancing. Night has fallen, and the end of the fair dance is now in full swing. Luis and I watch the couples on the dance floor moving rhythmically in time to the music. Nat had to go home a few minutes ago, so now it's just the two of us. It's too bad she had to leave now. Apparently, they will be having some fireworks go off after the dance is over and I'm really looking forward to seeing that.

From where I am standing, I am watching Shay dance with a young man who I believe is her boyfriend who just arrived in town today. She is wearing her tiara from the contest and is smiling broadly as she twirls across the dance floor. I am so glad that everything worked out so well for her. I hope that she can go back to all those big cities she goes to for modeling soon. She said that she was only in this competition to get money to go to college. If she was determined to stay in this contest when she was getting picked on so mercilessly by the other contestants, then she deserves to get the money she needs to go to college and follow her dreams. I can only admire someone with that level of dedication. I know that she will go far in life.

I see someone coming toward Luis and I that quickly ends my good mood, Alex. He walks straight up to me with a timid smile on his face, something I am not used to seeing on him. He usually looks very confident, no matter the situation he's in. He gives me a brief smile before he lowers his gaze.

"Hello Colomba."

"Alex." I say rather coldly, hoping that he will take a hint and leave me alone. He does not.

"Can I talk to you for a minute, alone?" I notice Luis stiffen in anger.

"If you want to talk to me you can say what you please here." Anger flashes in Alex's eyes for a moment as he looks at Luis, but he goes back to his timid appearance as soon as his gaze returns to me.

"I just wanted to say that I am sorry for the way I have been acting over the past few days. I have been a real jerk and I hope that you can forgive me." I cross my arms over my chest.

"I wasn't the one you hurt by what you did. You should apologize to Luis." Both Alex and Luis look over at me with surprise. Alex looks from me to Luis and back again awkwardly, as if trying to make a decision. Apparently, he makes his decision since he faces Luis.

"Luis, I am sorry for the way I've been acting. Do you forgive me?" Alex almost growls this, as if it is literally painful for him to apologize to Luis. Luis glares down at him. Even though Luis is taller than Alex by quite a few inches, Alex somehow seems to stand taller, as if his confidence makes him seem more formidable.

"I forgive you." From his tone, I can tell that Luis doesn't really forgive Alex. He is merely saying it out of politeness. I can understand how he feels. I would find it very difficult to forgive someone who purposefully tries to embarrass you in front of your friends. Now that he has Luis' apology, Alex smiles at me with his usual confident grin.

"Well, since we are all on good terms now, how would you like to have a dance with me? I believe they will be closing up soon so we should dance while we can." I want to yell at him because I am so furious right now. It is pretty obvious what he is doing. He just apologized to Luis just to get on my good side and have things go back to normal, but that's not happening. I am not going to let myself be tricked by him, I will not deal with him and his constant showing off and flirting anymore. I made a mistake. I thought that I was being kind by talking to him and everything, but I was really just being a push over. You don't have to be friends with everyone to be a kind person, it is alright to create boundaries with people who aren't worthy of being your friend. I don't have to deal with this in my life.

I look at Alex with his confident grin and handsome face. I think about the many conversations we have had together that he practically controlled, and all the time we have spent together mainly in PE class. I think about all of that and I let it go. I don't need him and his negative influence in my life. I don't have time to deal with that kind of mess.

"I'm sorry Alex, but I have already promised to give the last dances to Luis." I smile at Luis who is staring down at me in shock. The shock quickly fades to be replaced by a sweet smile. I think he understands what I am doing. I am trying to get away from Alex and this uncomfortable situation, and I am taking him with me. He gently takes my hand and leads me onto the dancefloor where a slower song is beginning to play. Luis holds me close as we start swaying in time to the music, a happy smile on his face.

"Thanks for dancing with me Luis. I really needed to get away from him."

"I understand. I'm just glad that you now see him the way everybody else does."

"Yeah, I just wish that I had realized it sooner." I lower my eyes from his, suddenly feeling ashamed. "Luis, I'm sorry I didn't believe you when you tried to warn me about Alex a few months ago. You tried to tell me that he only cared about me because he thinks I'm pretty and that he is mean to everyone else. I didn't believe you then and I got mad at you even though you were trying to protect me. I'm sorry." He smiles down at me, no anger in his eyes at my past mistake.

"It's alright. You thought he was your friend. It's hard to think badly of a friend. I just… I just really hope that you won't let him back in your life." Just from looking at his face I can tell that he truly is afraid that I will be friends with Alex again. What has Alex done to Luis in the past to make Luis so afraid of him now? I don't think Luis wants to tell me about any of that, so I won't ask him.

"Trust me, that won't be happening any time soon. To be honest, he was kind of annoying to be around anyway." Luis laughs a bit unexpectedly. "I mean it, he really was. All he would ever talk about was himself and he was always showing off about stuff. He was also always flirting with me and it was really irritating, and it also made me super uncomfortable most of the time. I didn't want to just ditch him though because I just didn't want to be mean to someone who was being kind to me. It didn't seem right."

"I'm glad." He is definitely telling the truth about being glad. Luis is practically glowing with happiness right now. I can't say that thought about Alex. Alex is still standing where Luis and I left him, staring at the two of us in surprise and rage. There is so much anger in his gaze that I am almost frightened. If looks could kill, Luis and I would be a pile of ash right now. His gaze full of hatred is mainly directed toward Luis though, so I might just be severely burned instead of ash.

I've always had the suspicion that Luis and Alex really don't like each other, but what is shown in Alex's eyes is beyond dislike, even beyond hatred. What is in Alex's eyes is the most frightening thing I've ever seen, and I just fought a super powered girl who transformed people into monsters. There is something about that glare that just sends a shiver down my spine. There is something in that glare that tells me that Alex really wants to hurt Luis. As if Luis is a monster that needs to be slain.

I won't let that happen though. I won't let Luis leave my sight until this night is over and I know that he is safely back home. I won't let Alex hurt my friend. I have a strong feeling that he has already hurt Luis many times over the years, but I won't let it happen anymore. I will protect my friend even if that means that I get hurt in the process. If Alex even tries to do anything to Luis, he will finally understand just how frightening I can be. He has always doubted what I am able to do because of my small size, but if he tries to hurt my friend he will find out just how much I can hurt him.

Luis and I dance for several songs in a row, neither of us even mentioning stopping. He twirls me around the dancefloor and it almost feels like we are dancing on a cloud. I have never taken dance lessons before, but Luis has told me about how both of his parents were dance instructors before they died. They obviously passed their talent down to their son. He seems to dance as if he was born knowing how. I never expected someone as shy or as large as Luis to be so graceful. Luis has always appeared a bit clumsy to me. He is very tall and lank, but his hands and feet are very big, so I think that he has a lot more growing to do. He always seems to be tripping over his own feet, but when he's on the dancefloor it feels a lot different. He appears so sure of his own movements. I'm kind of impressed. Luis isn't very confident with most things, but ever since I've met him, he's become more and more confident with his artistic abilities. I suppose I have just found another one of his artistic talents.

We dance until the final song of the night is played. Only then do we separate. I look over to see that Alex is still glaring at Luis. I smile up at Luis.

"Hey, I think we have a little bit of time before the fair closes. Is there one last ride you would like to go on?" He smiles down at me and doesn't even stop to think before he gives me his answer. An answer that I really didn't expect.

"Let's go on the Ferris Wheel."

# Chapter Eighteen
## Luis-
## The Ferris
## Wheel

Colomba and I race through the crowd to make it to the Ferris Wheel. With my longer legs, I am beating her in the race, but with her athleticism she is only a hair behind me. The two of us laugh with joy as we finally make it to the Ferris Wheel. We only have to wait for a moment before the guy in charge of the ride lets us on. As we take our seats in the Ferris Wheel, I pull a small box out of my pocket while the Ferris Wheel starts to take us up into the air.

"Hey Colomba, I have something that I wanted to give you. Just something small to thank you for modeling for me for the portrait." Colomba smiles softly at me.

"Luis, you didn't have to get me anything. I

was happy to do it for you." I smile too, knowing that she means what she said. She was happy to help me.

"Yeah, but I saw how much you liked this, and I thought that it would be perfect." She opens the little box, and her smile deepens when she sees that inside the box is the necklace that she had loved so much but couldn't afford. "Oh Luis, thank you. Can you help me put it on?" I take the necklace from her hand as she turns herself around and lifts up her hair so that I can wrap the necklace around her throat and fasten it. As soon as it is on, she looks down to admire it. "Luis, thank you. You are so sweet."

"You're welcome." I try to think of something else to say, but the Ferris Wheel suddenly stops with us near the very top and the screeching of a firework sailing through the sky echoes through the air before it explodes in a shower of bright colors. Colomba looks at the world above us as the fireworks explode, her eyes wide in childlike wonder.

"It's so beautiful." I know that she is referring to all the fireworks going off above us, but I only look at her as I make my reply.

"Yeah, beautiful." Her hand is resting on the bench between us. I want to hold her hand so badly. Lifting my hand off my lap, I reach toward her and then quickly pull it back again. I can't, I can't do it. I turn my attention away from her to look up at the fireworks display. Even though this is a picture-perfect moment to tell her how I feel like how Nat, and practically everyone else, has been telling me to do, I can't. It's hard to trust someone with your heart when it has already been broken countless times by other people.

Instead of saying what I wish to say, I simply watch the fireworks with her, glad that we can have this moment together.

# Chapter Nineteen
## Colomba-
## Why Now

My entire body aches in my exhaustion, but I am not upset by that. I have had too good of a time tonight to be upset by anything. I take the necklace that Luis gave me off and place it on my bedside table. I glance over to my dresser where the purple poodle is that Alex gave me the other day. I only look at it for a moment before I go over to it, pick it up, and toss it into my closet. I make sure that the door is firmly closed behind me so that I won't have to look at that thing again tonight. I'll make sure to donate it tomorrow so that somebody can have some joy from it since I surely will never feel any joy even looking at it. The only thing I will ever think about when I see that purple poodle would be Alex, and I don't want to think of him ever again.

What I really need to think about right now is the Crow and what is going on with him. Why did he disappear for a couple months after what happened with the Black Iris? Why did he reappear now? And why did he choose to make Shay his next victim?

Maybe he disappeared after that because he felt bad that I had defeated him so many times and he felt like giving up. Maybe he just wanted a break. Or maybe he wanted some time to plan for something big against me.

Maybe he has appeared now because it was the fair and he knew that he would have a lot more people to scare than usual at the school. Or maybe he thought that it would just be more dramatic to make his come back at the fair. He does seem like the kind of guy who likes being dramatic.

And when it comes to the question of why he chose Shay, I don't think I have a guess. To know that she was having problems with the other girls would mean that he has some kind of connection to either Shay, the contest, or one of the other girls who were competing. As to which one of those choices is the answer, I won't even bother to guess. With all of the assumptions I have been making, I know that I should just give up on guessing. I will never find the real answer that way, and even if I do guess correctly I won't know if it's true or not because I can't just go up to the Crow and ask him if I'm right or not.

Instead of thinking about questions that I can never answer, I think about everything that happened tonight. After everything with the Beauty Queen died down, it was no surprise that Shay won the contest by a landslide. What made me even happier though was watching the look of surprise and joy on Luis' face when he found out that he had won the portrait contest. I am so proud of him. He really did deserve to win that prize money. It was really touching that he spent some of that prize money to get me that necklace I had loved so much. Luis is such a thoughtful guy.

It felt so nice to dance with him too and to end the night watching the fireworks display. Everyone was just so happy at the fair. I never wanted it to end. I want happy moments like this to happen all the time for everyone, but there are many things that stand in the way of people being happy. One of the big reasons right now is the Crow.

If the Crow thinks that he can come back and I won't stand in his way, then he's sure going to be surprised. I will fight harder than before. I won't back down. I will make him feel terror at the mention of my name. I will make him fear the very sight of me. I will make him surrender if it is the last thing I do.

# Chapter Twenty
## Luis-
## One Final
## Question

I lift my hands over my head in a massive stretch as I take in a big yawn. I'm exhausted, yet I still don't want to sleep. I don't want this day to end. I set down the finished picture of the Beauty Queen that I just drew in my sketchbook and put it in my desk drawer.

Shadow is carefully using her beak to straighten out her feathers on my bed. I guess that's a crow's way of preparing for the night just like how people brush their teeth before going to bed. I carefully place my prize money on top of my dresser so that I can remember to bring it with me to the art supply store so I can get my painting stuff. I am so excited about trying out painting. I've only really been able to afford doing sketches since that is probably one of the cheapest art forms out there. All you need is some paper and a pencil. As I go over what I want to paint first I hear Shadow speaking behind me.

"I'm sorry that your plans for the Beauty Queen didn't work out." I smile back at her.

"Don't be sorry Shadow. I think it worked out pretty well. I mean Shay won the contest, she made all those girls stop picking on her real quick after she transformed them into those creepy little monsters, I won a couple ribbons and a bunch of prize money, and I got to dance with Colomba and watch the fireworks with her. It was a pretty great return as the Crow even if Silver Dove did defeat me in the end. Who cares if the Beauty Queen got defeated? We both got what we wanted." Shadow nods her head.

"I understand, but I know that you had been preparing for this for months and you were hoping that it would be your final battle to change everything and-"

"Shadow, please." I interrupt her, not wanting to hear about my failure anymore. "It's happened, it's over. Let's just change the subject, shall we?" Shadow nods again.

"Alright then, what happened to your mission of asking Colomba to the dance?" I lower my head, not wanting to look at Shadow. Out of every subject she could have chosen for a conversation, she had to choose that one.

"Things just… happened, I got distracted. With everything going on with the Beauty Queen, isn't it natural that I had other things on my mind besides that?" I hear Shadow flapping her wings, and it doesn't surprise me when I feel her land on my shoulder.

"Is that really the excuse you are going to use

with me?" I look at her, completely confused.

"What do you mean Shadow?" She shakes her head at me.

"Do you expect me to believe that Master?" I stare at her with wide eyes, surprised that she is saying this to me in such a harsh tone. "You had every opportunity to ask her, but you didn't. You were scared."

"I was not scared!" I force myself to calm down, knowing that my uncle is just downstairs and it would seem pretty weird for him to hear me yelling when he thinks that there is nobody else here. "Things just happened, I wasn't scared of asking her." Shadow narrows her eyes at me in frustration.

"Master, you know that I can listen to your heart. I know exactly how you felt. You were afraid of asking her and that held you back. You let your fears get in the way of what you wanted to do. That is the surest way to have many regrets in life. If you are always denying why you didn't do something you wanted then you will never be truly happy. There will always be something to stand in your way." I lower my eyes again, feeling ashamed. I know I have to tell the truth now. Shadow knows me far too well to try and lie again.

"Okay, maybe I was scared, alright? It's hard to not be scared when you want to ask somebody to a dance. I wanted to go with her, but I just couldn't ask her and then everything got crazy with the Beauty Queen. I just…"

"You just what Master?" I sigh, feeling completely defeated.

"I just wish I wasn't so afraid all the time." Shadow uses her beak to push my long bangs out of my eyes.

"Don't worry. One day you will wake up and realize that the painful time in your life is over and a time of happiness has begun. Once you realize that, the fear will begin to leave you because then you will feel safe." I look into her sympathetic, black eyes.

"When will that time come though?" Shadow lowers her eyes from mine, probably not wanting to see the pitiful look in my gaze.

"Nobody can ever tell. The future holds many unexpected things, and nothing is set in stone. All we can do is keep moving forward and working hard so that we can have a better tomorrow." I laugh softly at how ridiculous I am about to sound with what needs to be said.

"I guess I'm just afraid that I'm going to always be alone." Shadow's black eyes stare deep into my gaze and I know that she wants to me to keep talking, to explain what I mean. "I've been alone almost my entire life. Even though I was alone, I wasn't lonely. It's hard to be lonely when you've always been alone. I guess that's because if you're always alone you don't really have anything to compare it to. Now that I have been friends with Colomba and Nat, I understand what it's like to be lonely. I feel it when they're not around and I am stuck with the people who constantly hurt me, like Alex. I'm afraid that one day my new friends will leave me once they realize just how much of a loser I am, and I will be alone forever. I'm always afraid that I will be alone."

"It is a natural fear to be alone. Humans are social creatures. No matter what anybody says, humans need each other to survive. To be truly alone is one of the worst things that could ever happen to anyone. What matters though is that you did dance with her. She may have been the one to ask you, but you got what you were hoping for. That is a good sign, she wanted to dance with you. Maybe one day you will find the courage and ask her out, but until then I see hope for the two of you." I smile at her, trying to forget the pain and misery I had felt only moments before.

"Thanks Shadow. Let's do something else for right now. I don't want to think about all that anymore. I'm going to turn on the TV and relax before going to bed." I flop down on my bed and use the remote to turn on the television. Within a flash, the news comes on to show a picture of the Beauty Queen and Silver Dove duking it out next to the newscaster. The scene looks as if it was filmed on some bystander's phone. I sit up straight, my attention immediately grabbed.

"It is still unclear as to why the Crow has decided to return at this time, but as per usual, Silver Dove was able to defeat him. The person who became his victim today, a young woman by the name of Shay Montgomery, has already been questioned about her experience by the police and has been ordered not to give any information regarding the experience to anyone else at this time." Well that's strange. The police never required that of anybody else I have transformed before. I think back on what I saw on the news the other day. They were talking about new procedures that the school has set up just in case the Crow attacks the school again. I guess the town has set up a few as well. Hmm… I guess the people running the school and town aren't as dumb as I thought. Well they will learn that no matter how much they prepare I cannot be stopped by any normal human being. The only one who can stop me is the only other person who has a pin like mine, Silver Dove.

She may think that she's winning, but she's wrong. Nobody dares to mess with the kids that I have transformed anymore. They are able to live peaceful, happy lives now because of me. They were able to get their revenge and show everyone that they have strength hidden inside, I just helped it come out. All the other kids know that if they dare to mess with those same kids again, then I will just have to transform them again and they will regret it.

Silver Dove thinks that she's the one making things better for these guys. She couldn't be more wrong. How can she help all of these people I've given powers to just by talking to them? It doesn't make sense. She is stupid for thinking that a few words can change anything for someone. It takes force to make things change. It's the only thing that works in this world.

The new school year starts in just a few days. I will be a sophomore this year. I won't waste my time like I did last year. I won't waste time asking myself what-if questions or thinking about what will happen. I will just do what I feel needs to be done. Eventually I will end my crusade, but only once the world realizes that it can't hurt the weak anymore. Not while I'm around that is. I am here to protect the weak, and the world has already been warned. They have been warned yet they keep harming other people like me. The world just needs to be taught a harsh lesson, and I am willing to teach it.

Eliza Scalia is a therapist who has a Masters degree in Clinical Mental Health from Troy University. She enjoys reading, writing, and needlework, as well as hanging out with her pet cat, Dusty. Eliza has been writing since she was in middle school and has self- published the Death's Assistant series for young adults.

www.ingramcontent.com/pod-product-compliance
Lightning Source LLC
Chambersburg PA
CBHW070512200726
48293CB00007B/2491